I0557144

Your Desire

Dee S. Knight

Nomad Authors Publishing

Your Desire
by Dee S. Knight

Copyright © 2020 by Dee S. Knight
Cover design by Francis Drake

Nomad Authors Publishing
https://www.nomadauthors.com
ISBN 978-1-7347610-1-6

Dedicated!

This book is for you, sweetheart, because you always have filled my life with magic. I love you!

Contents

Dee S. Knight

Prologue

The whir of a sewing machine traveled across the ether. As intended, the sound blended with the those of a lawn mower in Cleveland, a blender in Dallas, an electric razor in Seattle. Some people, those specially attuned to properties outside the normal realm of humans, heard buzzing that *could* have been a sewing machine, but it was faint and truly indistinguishable for what it was. More like a mosquito at the ear. They heard it but couldn't decipher exactly where to swat, so they did their best ignore it.

Of course, the sound was not *supposed* to be heard, and therefore not investigated. The very few who did hear it clearly, who also heard Nigel and his granddaughter clearly, well, they generally resided in a hospital setting where three squares a day were provided and tranquility came in the form of little green pills. At the least, they saw a shrink three times a week. Their knowledge wasn't taken seriously.

This worried Nigel, but what could he do? It wasn't his fault humans had devolved to the point where they no longer believed in enchantment. He shook his head and *tsked* as he sewed. When he was a boy learning the business from his grandfather as his granddaughter now learned from him, no one would have believed the universe could get to this point, where people believed in the "magic" of technology but not the magic that could be found in their own hearts.

Of course, challenges were exciting, and skeptical humans certainly kept him on his toes.

Absently, he hummed as he completed the final seam on the full, purple satin skirt. He pulled it from the machine, snipped the threads and shook the material out before pinning it on the dress form.

"Edwina! I have the skirt finished. Come here, dear." Standing back to cast a critical eye over how the skirt hung, he held up an artist's rendition of what the final product should be. He looked from drawing to garment, made a few small adjustments to the pleating around the waist and nodded in satisfaction.

"Hey, Gramps," his granddaughter said, bounding into the room.

For the millionth time, he mentally cringed at the lack of style in today's youth. Their kind had the ability to appear any way they wished. Glancing in the mirror, he saw a debonair David Niven reflected back. The sleeves of his snowy white shirt were rolled to his elbows, but the Windsor knot in his tie was perfect, as was the knife-sharp crease in his trousers and the shine on his shoes. When he rolled down his sleeves and put on his jacket, he would look every inch the gentleman. Quirking his brows in approval, he unconsciously ran a fingertip lightly over his moustache. Instead of selecting what he would consider an appropriate shell, Edwina—a name which screamed propriety—chose to look like a bag lady gone wild.

Like today, for instance. Long blond hair, streaked with pink and purple, pulled up into a ponytail to hang down the side of her head. Black lipstick and eye shadow. Two earrings in one ear and four in the other. A bright orange tank top and faded jeans—separated scandalously by a good three inches of bare stomach—looked as though they'd been worn (and torn) for centuries. And her feet—her lovely, dainty feet!—

were shod in horrid, ugly brown things that not even the most desperate soldier in Caesar's army would have donned.

When he had questioned her once about her appearance, she'd said with delight that she was starting her own trend. A Lauper-Madonna-Pink look. It was *not* something he'd understood. Today, after a quick perusal, he leaned closer.

"What is *that*?" He swiped his thumb across her cheek, then examined what was on the pad.

"Body glitter. Isn't it cool?" She grinned at him.

Her enthusiasm, as well as her utter lack of self-consciousness, brought the slightest of smiles to his eyes, even as his mouth formed a moue of reproach.

"Yes, well." He wiped his thumb on a handkerchief pulled from the pocket of his jacket, hanging on the wall behind Edwina. "'Cool' is what ice cubes provide. I don't know what body glitter is good for."

Giggles flowed from her, reminding him of when she was a small girl instead of the nearly grown youngster she was now. Where *had* the centuries gone? Despite the shudders her wardrobe caused, he loved Edwina enormously and strove to give her the very best education in what they did, which was make dreams come true.

To his amazement, she stood on tiptoe and kissed his cheek. "I love you, Gramps!"

Blushing with pleasure, he patted her shoulder. "As I do you, my dear. Now, however" —briskly he turned back to the skirt falling in soft folds to brush the floor—"we must perform our first infusion of magic."

He glanced to see if Edwina was listening with the proper attention and she rewarded him with a serious expression. "The first layer of magic is performed now, as the garment is being made. The next layer is cast—"

"When the pieces are put together," she finished.

He beamed. "Very good. The final layer is added with adornments, like the lace, pearls and beads you'll sew on the bodice of this dress. Do you know the chant?"

"Yes, Gramps."

"Excellent. Remember, the chant must be said for each bauble sewn, so that the spell isn't lessened if a bead is lost."

"I'll remember." She reached to touch the dress. "You don't usually work from a picture. Why this time?"

Nigel laid the drawing on the cutting table. "Because our Ms. Meadows will need to see the drawing in order to be convinced."

"It's beautiful, and when we're finished it will be a gorgeous gown. The woman who buys this one will be very lucky."

"Oh, this dress isn't for sale. This is for the mannequin in the window."

"We're going to all this work for a dress that won't even be worn?" She turned a wide-eyed gaze on him.

"I didn't say it won't be worn." He dusted non-existent lint from his hands, rolled his sleeves down and slid his arms into his jacket. "Now. We don't have much more time before we arrive in San Francisco, so take my hand and let's say our incantation."

With one hand each on the material and the others joined, they recited the words used to fuse magic into the seams of the skirt. For a brief moment the space of air around the skirt glowed blue. Then it looked as though nothing had happened. They dropped hands and stepped back.

"Very nice, Edwina. You've learned the spells well. I'm *quite* proud of you."

She smiled, pleasure obvious in the sparkle of her eyes.

Giving her shoulder a squeeze he added, "As I said, there's much left to do before we appear on Post Street. We'd better get to work."

Picking up a packet of pins, she followed him to the cutting table and they started

Dee S. Knight

The Artist and the Director

Dee S. Knight

Chapter One

Derica Meadows strolled down Post Street on her way back from lunch. It was Friday afternoon, and with all of her work caught up, she was seriously considering taking off early. Her firm's annual bash, presented for their clients, was being held the next night, and since she had to put in extra hours to schmooze then, there was no reason to feel guilty about taking a few hours for herself now. But it still took some self-convincing.

Derica's employer, MiBar Medical, produced and sold medical devices, which ensured the guest list would be jammed with doctors and other representatives from the medical field, as well as with the full complement of MiBar's managerial staff. The party was a formal affair with dinner and dancing. She mused lazily that she could claim the time to prepare. After all, she hadn't decided which of her several dressy pantsuits to wear. Picking a color wasn't difficult—they were all black. But she hadn't yet decided whether to go with lace-trimmed or plain, tailored or relaxed, or how she might add the trademark splash of bright color she used for accent. *A new scarf might be nice.*

Looking for something bright to catch her eye, she glanced in the shops that lined the street. Unlike some women who didn't like wearing the same outfit twice, Derica didn't let the thought bother her. After all, men wore the same tuxedo year after year. That is, if they didn't gain too much weight, and then they rented one just like the old one. Why should she spend a lot of money on something new when the style and accent piece changed the look quite enough?

15

Food would be plentiful and liquor would flow, and by ten o'clock some of the men would be drunk enough to hit on anything in a skirt. Since she didn't appreciate the "honor," wearing pants sometimes helped alleviate any problems before she had to finesse her way out of an unpleasant situation. Derica didn't try for sexy, she just tried to make it through the evening. A slip of etiquette—or decorum—on an evening like this, and a woman's whole career could be shot all to hell. That wouldn't happen to her. She kept herself squarely within the guidelines of corporate expectations at all times. It was best.

She dreaded the corporate gatherings, but for someone in her position—management and moving up—they were required. Five years ago, when she'd started at MiBar, parties had been something fun, something to look forward to. But for the past couple of years, time spent socializing for the job had become a chore.

First, she had to find a man to accompany her. This was difficult only because she was so determined to get ahead that she was very fussy about the type of man she dated. If she'd simply wanted to go out, finding a date wouldn't be hard—she was honest enough to admit she was no slouch in the looks department—but ambition forced her to pay strict attention to her escort. She took care to make sure he was sophisticated and looked professional. Someone who could converse with the men and charm the wives, but in a non-threatening way. It wasn't always an easy slot to fill.

For this party, she was in a spot. Her usual companion, her friend Randy, was out of town. She'd tried and failed to talk her brother into escorting her. It looked to be a repeat performance of what had happened one other year when she'd found being unescorted brought on veiled passes and innuendo, both from clients and some of her colleagues.

Next, she had to battle the self-appointed fashion squad, composed of The Wives of the most senior management. *Frankly, I'd rather fend off the groping hands of their husbands on the dance floor than face the women who dictate proper length, style and color of my dress.* She'd solved that problem with her classy black suits, designed to look good and fit comfortably. They weren't particularly feminine. Certainly they weren't revealing or seductive in any way. And that seemed to satisfy The Wives.

Last was the sheer boredom of the party itself. There were no surprises anymore, no sparks. She kept her wits about her by hardly drinking, but for the last few parties she'd wished she could let loose. She never would, of course. Sadly, she wasn't a "let loose" sort of woman and her position was too important to her.

Derica snapped out of her daze when she found herself staring at a satin gown in a shop window. The glass must have been old and wavy because everything in the display looked distorted. With her head in one position, the dress appeared to be deep purple and the trumpet beads adorning the laced bodice looked huge. Leaning a few inches in the opposite direction, the folds of satin took on the palest shade of lavender, diffused to the point she had to stare to ensure it *was* lavender instead of washed of color. Then the trumpet beads were barely noticeable. Instead she was struck with the intricate pattern of seed pearls gracing the top and the capped sleeves.

With a huff of frustration at not being able to get a sharp view, she was compelled to go inside so she could inspect the garment without the filter of glass.

Your Desire. The name was painted on the door in simple block print. She pulled the handle and stepped into the cramped store, where she came face to face with an older, prim man in a well-worn suit. Gray touched his temples but not his thin moustache. His dark brown eyes warmed her to her core, and she felt immediate trust in him.

The shop didn't inspire such trust, however. It was on the shabby side of shabby-chic, and like the man's suit, had seen better days. That explained why she hadn't noticed the place before—it wasn't the sort of establishment in which she usually shopped.

"May I help you?" the man asked.

She turned toward the window display. *What the hell!* The effect remained the same. The satin seemed to change shades of purple depending on her position. One way she noticed the beads, another she saw the pearls. Now she saw barely visible lines of sequins between folds of the skirt. Although there was no breeze, the skirt seemed to shift, and tiny shards of light shot from the sequins otherwise hidden in the yards of material.

"Yes, that dress in the window, I've never seen anything like it."

"It *is* unique, part of our special collection." He sounded proud. "May we make one like it for you?"

"Make one?" She stepped forward and reached out. The touch of her fingers caused swirls of violet to run through the fabric from waist to hem, and she gasped as she jerked her hand away. "No, I need the dress for tomorrow night." Curious, she faced the man. "I can't believe you made this. It's wonderful!"

He closed his eyes and graciously nodded his acknowledgement.

The mannequin in the window drew her attention again. She'd never owned anything so soft and feminine. Suddenly her black pantsuits seemed totally unsuitable for the office party, dull and lifeless, even when she imagined them paired with a bright scarf or lacy camisole.

"How much for this dress?" Damn! She'd failed to keep intense interest from her voice. If she were the salesperson, she'd immediately jack up the price.

"Oh, you don't want that. It's only for display and very old. I can't guarantee your satisfaction."

Slowly Derica turned to the man, her mind turning over possibilities of why he wouldn't want to take advantage of a sale. Did he think to haggle and increase the price, now that she'd shown her excitement? Well, if that was his game, she could play, too.

"Perhaps you're right. I have a formal affair tomorrow night. Do you have anything else?" Casting a glance at the drab interior, she carefully kept her expression neutral. "I'm a size eight," she offered, seeing him give her an appraising look.

He nodded. "That's exactly what I would have said. If you'll follow me, I think we have just what you're looking for."

They walked to the back of the store and through a curtained doorway. There she found a softly lighted alcove with two stuffed chairs on either side of a dark-stained piecrust table. A cup of steaming tea and a plate of shortbread were on a tray. She examined the room in amazement, not having expected a showroom. In fact, she'd barely expected curtains on the dressing rooms, based on the appearance of the shop.

"Just make yourself comfortable, and we'll see what we have, shall we?" He waved her into one of the chairs then turned toward another, smaller doorway to her side. "Edwina, we're ready."

A young woman dramatically swept aside the material covering the entryway and emerged wearing a pink chiffon formal with a fitted bodice and long sleeves. What caught Derica's attention however, was the woman's shape. She could have been Derica's body double with her long legs, narrow, rounded hips, and tiny waist. The woman's breasts would have nicely filled out Derica's own B-cup bra. The difference came in her beautiful violet eyes and heart shaped, Kewpie doll lips, painted bright red.

And also in her short spiked hair that was a most interesting shade of yellow. Derica was so taken with their similarities in shape, it didn't occur to her to wonder why the woman was poised and ready to model formal gowns.

"This is my granddaughter, Edwina." The man beamed at Edwina then turned his warm smile on Derica. "And I'm Nigel Brown."

"I'm Derica Meadows. That's a lovely gown, Mr. Brown," she said, as the woman twirled to show off the flow of the skirt. "But it looks like something for a prom."

His smile fell ever so slightly. "Oh, dear. Well, Edwina…" He shooed her behind the curtain.

After what felt like only seconds, Edwina came out again, wearing a lime green skirt and white ruffled blouse.

"No, that's not right at all. I need something for a company dinner, and I want a gown that will knock everyone back on their heels."

She'd barely taken a sip of tea before Edwina left and came back, this time in a sleek black sheath that displayed too much leg on one end and far too much cleavage on the other. Derica cringed then smiled, thinking of the reactions of The Wives if she wore this dress to the party. But a sexy little number wasn't what she wanted. She wanted mystery underlying a thoroughly feminine sophistication.

She wanted the dress in the window.

Nigel looked at Edwina and opened his mouth to say something— probably to tell her to try something else—but Derica stopped him. "Mr. Brown, let me speak frankly. You've shown me lovely dresses but the only thing I've seen that interests me is the dress in the window. If you're not prepared to let me buy it…?" She shrugged her shoulders. "Then I'm afraid I have no business here. So, will you entertain a purchase, or not?"

Pursing his lips and tapping his mouth with his forefinger, Nigel stood silent. Edwina disappeared behind the curtain and then moments later passed through the showroom and into the shop, dressed in heeled, dark brown leather boots, a mid-calf length brown suede skirt and high-necked white blouse. *How does she do that?* But Derica didn't have time to ponder the question further.

"Would you be willing to pay two hundred dollars as a deposit? As I mentioned, it is one of a kind and I'd hate to lose the only pattern I have." Nigel spoke without a trace of indecisiveness. Derica admired a person who took the bull by the horns once they'd made a decision.

"Two hundred dollars as a deposit? That amount won't give me ownership?" Two hundred was a steal to buy the thing, but to rent it? He was a canny businessman after all.

"Let's call it a lease. If you return it undamaged by the end of the month, and you've been satisfied with the results, your money will be refunded."

She narrowed her eyes. "I've never heard of any store doing this kind of thing."

He waved his hand. "We're not like any other store you've frequented, Ms. Meadows. Can't you tell that?"

In fact, he was right. There was something different about this shop. Shabby but sophisticated. Quick change artists and enchanting dresses. There was a sense of something unworldly.

"Suppose something happens to the dress. What would I owe then?"

He looked at her, his eyes twinkling. "The gown itself is priceless, as I believe you've already proven. When someone wants an item as much as you want that dress, well, is there a price too high? However, I think this arrangement will work out fine."

His eyes captured her total attention. They blazed with power and knowledge. Deep, ancient knowledge. She couldn't turn away.

Then they softened. "If that dress is what you want, you should accept my offer. I assure you, there is no other like it in all the world."

"Will it fit, do you think?" Her voice was barely above a whisper.

"You're a perfect size eight. It's a perfect size eight. For you, the gown will be...perfect." He ended with a smile as warm as a summer day, and she smiled back.

"Will you accept a check?"

He nodded. "Of course."

Shaking her head slightly at the strangeness of the deal and the suddenness with which they'd completed it, she preceded Nigel from the room. He then took the lead, taking her to a small counter where Edwina stood, securing a handle onto a large box. She looked at her grandfather.

"Ms. Meadows has agreed to pay two hundred dollars, Edwina, and will return the gown to us by the end of the month."

Without a scintilla of surprise Edwina turned her gaze from her grandfather to Derica. "I'm afraid we don't accept credit cards."

She indicated the cash register, the oldest Derica had ever seen. In fact, she didn't know if she had ever seen a manual machine such as this one.

"We haven't exactly embraced the twenty-first century," Edwina continued.

"I see that," murmured Derica.

In moments it seemed, Derica found herself on the sidewalk outside the shop, holding a large dress box. The mannequin in the front window now sported a heavy wool coat with fur-trimmed collar. She snorted. That was an odd thing to advertise in San Francisco, and wondered again at the man's sense of business. *She'd* never hire him, that was for sure. Imagine leasing a dress! The gown was worth hundreds of dollars, and she'd given him a measly two hundred. And in cash, too. She was honest, of course, and would bring the dress back, but a good many people wouldn't.

Turning away, Derica barely noticed the old woman staring with longing at the coat in the window. Nor did the tinkle of the bell on the door make an impression as the woman entered the store.

Your Desire

Dee S. Knight

Chapter Two

Derica virtually sailed into the lobby of the sumptuous downtown hotel, her usual confident posture becoming an almost regal bearing. It was the dress that changed her attitude, the flowing satin and lace, the beads and pearls, and knowing that the sequins caught rays of light from the lobby chandeliers and flashed them back as she took each step. Without even looking, she knew every eye was on her as she made her entrance, and it was a heady experience.

She stopped at the directory to find the location of the MiBar event, and saw her reflection in the glass of the case. Her normally short black hair appeared long and upswept, thanks to the genius of her hairdresser. The finger she put to the glass to search for the correct room was shaped and polished in the lightest shade of lavender. Funny how a simple manicure could change a girl's whole outlook! Rather than the professional woman, her softly shaded violet eye shadow and frosted light pink lipstick reflected a woman who was completely feminine but who knew how to use her femininity in bold and powerful ways. A woman who was *hot*.

This woman didn't mind attending the party alone because she was certain not to be alone long. There was a certain thrill in that thought. Oh, she wouldn't be interested in attracting any of the married men, but the woman staring back at her might have fun throwing out a few lures to the single guys who happened to be there. There was a strange stirring in her to let loose and live large for a change. Reach for a brass ring she'd never noticed before. The urge to do something different—be someone different—had never been so strong.

The Wives, expecting the normal Derica-in-Black-Pantsuit, would be scandalized by her look and the aura of womanly force she projected, but they'd have to get over it. Tonight she was Deri, not Derica, flirt and vamp, not conservative, cautious executive, a seeker of adventure, not a practical "do what it takes to get ahead" follower. No, tonight she would throw caution to the wind!

Frowning at the woman in the glass, she revised that. She'd throw caution to the wind within *reason*.

Maybe she'd toss a *tiny* bit of prudence to the breeze. After all, this was just a party and only for this one night. She didn't want anything that happened in one night to affect the rest of her career. Or her life.

She nodded to her reflection, smiled and headed past the huge arrangement of flowers on a carved table in the center of the lobby. The bank of elevators was to the rear of the ornate, red-carpeted stairway, which was blocked by a horde of people around cameras and photographers' lights. Slowing only a bit, she picked her way through the crowd. It seemed these days film crews were everywhere, using the fabulous city views as backdrop for their work. She spared only a moment to wonder what this crew was filming.

"Hey, you!" A man's voice rang out from the other side of the stairway. "Stop, lady!"

Someone touched her arm as she tried to get by. "I think he wants you over there," a woman standing next to one of the lights said.

Derica looked up, puzzled. A burly man with thinning red hair and a fluffy auburn beard streaked with gray charged toward her, a frown on his face and anger in his eyes.

"Madeline Watson? Where in hell have you been? You've kept us waiting for twenty minutes. *Twenty minutes!* Do you know how much that costs?" He stepped back and gave her a quick look from head to toe.

"You've got me—"

"Hair's a little different but it's still okay. At least you're dressed and ready. That's one good thing. Get your butt over here so we can get started." He spun around and stomped off.

Derica stood her ground, wondering why he had her confused with someone else, but angry that he hadn't let her explain. It would serve him right if she just slipped away and didn't tell him anything. In fact, she turned to do just that when she felt him beside her again.

"Where are you going?" he practically bellowed. "We need you on this side of the stairway for lighting."

There wasn't a sound at that end of the lobby, as though everyone waited to see her reaction to him.

She drew herself to her full five foot ten inches and raised her head like the queen she'd felt herself to be earlier that evening. "I don't know who you think I am, but my name is *not* Madeline Watson."

The man closed his eyes and shook his head. "God spare me from temperamental actresses," he moaned. He looked at her. "Okay, so what's your name this week?" He waved his hands. "Never mind! We'll straighten it out with the agency *after the damn shoot*." His voice rose on the final words. "Now, come on."

Without the slightest attempt to listen to her protests, he grabbed her wrist and pulled her through the crowd that had surrounded them, to the other side of the lobby.

"Wait, damn it!"

Wrenching her arm from his hold, she stopped and glared at the man. He jammed his fists on his hips and glared back.

"I'm not who you think I am. My name's Derica Meadows, and I'm here for—"

"Samantha! Get over here and touch her up. And bring a contact and release form," he called over his shoulder, then he looked at her again. "Look lady," he started, weariness touching his voice, "I don't know what your name is, I really don't *care* what your name is, as long as we get it on the release form correctly. All I know is, you're wearing the dress, so you have to be the one the agency sent us." He thrust something into her hand then walked away.

Derica looked at the cardboard drawing. The woman portrayed could have been her. Slender, long neck, and black hair pulled up into an upsweep, although the style in the picture was different than hers. Actually, except for the hair style and color, the drawing looked like the girl at the dress shop. That girl...well, whatever her name was, it looked like her.

But the *dress*. The dress was a duplicate of what she wore, down to the sequins hidden on the skirt. The logical side of her brain tried to analyze what this was about. The man had told her the dress was old and one of a kind—an original he himself had made. Obviously, that wasn't true. What *was* true was that the drawing had the same appeal, the same magical, almost mystical sense about it.

"I'm so glad you finally got here," a young woman said as she ran her hands over Derica's hair, smoothing it and tucking in a few loose strands. "Ben has been beside himself."

Derica shrugged. "Look, I don't know who everyone thinks I am, but I'm not the person you're all waiting for."

The woman pursed her lips while she turned Derica's head toward the light. She whipped an eyeliner out of an opened case and ran it efficiently under Derica's eyes, then examined her work. With a satisfied nod, she took out a lip liner and worked on Derica's lips.

"You have to be the right person, don't you see? This dress is a designer original, one of a kind, made just for this campaign." With a finger of her free hand she tapped the drawing. "The dress is unique, you have on the dress, therefore you are the right person. Now purse your lips."

Derica did as she was ordered.

"Don't worry about Ben. That's the guy who yelled. He's just nervous because this is such a big account. And you *are* late. Okay, let me take another look."

Derica watched the woman stare at her face and then her body with a critical eye. She thrust a clipboard with a form on it into Derica's hand. "Here, honey, sign this while I finish up."

"What campaign is this anyway?" Derica dutifully filled in the blanks and signed, all the while uncertain why she did it.

The woman smoothed the waist of the dress and tugged the sleeves until they stood out from Derica's arms in perfect puffs. "The Violet Passion campaign." She frowned. "Jeez, something this big, you'd think the agency would tell you something. You know that romance novelist, Violet Sampson?"

"No, I don't read that stuff."

"Well, maybe you'll start after you get your first check from the campaign. You're beautiful and this is probably just the start for you." Professional and thorough, she continued inspecting, fluffing, and pulling on the dress as she spoke. "Anyway, she's a New York Times bestseller and she's branched out into perfumes. And maybe other stuff, if this is successful. This shoot is for the book cover and the TV trailers, but Ben hopes to sell them on the perfume label, too." She took the storyboard and gave Derica a nudge toward the stairs. "So get over there and break a leg!"

Looking around once more for someone to whom she could explain her predicament, Derica glanced up to the third step. And held her breath.

He was the most handsome man she'd ever seen. The old saying is that clothes make the man. Well, this guy wore a tuxedo that fit perfectly, but she had no illusion that it was the clothes making this guy. He'd look great even without the tux. Maybe *especially* without the tux.

People bustled around but all she saw was him, talking to another man standing one step below him. Hair as black as her own hung to the bottoms of his ears and touched his jaw, which was darkened with five o'clock shadow. She was too far away to see eye color, but she'd bet they were blue. Their intensity could be felt even though he wasn't looking directly at her. He looked trim and fit. The diamond stud in his ear winked through his raven black hair as he moved his head in conversation.

At that moment he looked up and met her eyes. She licked her lips.

A smile barely brushed his mouth. He said a few more words to the other man, but never took his eyes from her. When the other guy left, he slowly descended to the bottom step. Then he crooked his finger and bid her come the rest of the way to him.

And she did, as though she never had a choice.

She held out her hand. He took it in his larger one. His skin was cool, unlike his eyes, which blazed with heat. She sucked in a breath, certain that if it were her last she could die happy now that he'd touched her. Of course, now that he'd touched her, dying was the last thing she wanted to do. He pulled her closer as he stepped to the floor.

"My name is Kailen." He gave her a thorough male appraisal. "So this is the famous gown." He leaned to her ear. "The dress is beautiful, but you give it life."

Derica hardly knew what to say. She'd never been swept off her feet before, or so completely aroused by a simple touch or few words.

"I'm afraid this is all a mistake. I'm not supposed to be here at all." It was hard to speak over the noise her heart made with its wild beating.

A smile touched his lips and he gave her the same answer to her protest she'd heard since arriving. "No? But I'm sure you are. You're wearing the dress, after all." He didn't relinquish her hand. Instead, with a glance over her shoulder and a nod at someone behind her, he tucked it

33

into the crook of his elbow and turned her to the stairway. "Time to earn our keep," he said.

The chubby guy with the beard stormed up to them. "Okay, Kailen you've studied the boards and know what to do, right?"

Kailen nodded.

"And you, What's-Your-Name, the agency gave you the boards, right?"

Derica held up her hand to stop him from saying anything else. "Enough. There's been a mistake. I'm not the person you're expecting. I'm simply here to attend a company party upstairs in the Rosemont Room. I don't know who you think I am, but I'm not a model." There! She'd set him straight at last.

He stared at her for a few moments. "So the agency *didn't* get you the storyboards. That's great." He threw his hands into the air. "Of course! Why did I think this would be an easy shoot!"

"Didn't you hear me? I said—"

Kailen stepped forward, holding his hands up at Derica and Ben. "Ben, it's okay. Remember your blood pressure. I can show…" He looked at her questioningly.

"Derica," she supplied.

"I can show Derica what to do. Don't worry. It'll be fine."

With a glare at her and a look of resignation at Kailen, chubby Ben shook his head and walked away. "Get ready!" he yelled.

Blowing a breath, she looked up into Kailen's dark blue eyes. "Doesn't anyone listen to anything I say? I'm not a model. I'm not supposed to be in this commercial, or whatever it is."

"Look, maybe you're nervous or something. Is this your first job? Just relax. We know you're in the right place because you're—"

"Wearing the dress," they said in unison.

He smiled. "See? Now, you evidently didn't get the plans, so I'll tell you what to do. Go up about twenty steps and turn. When Ben calls 'Action!' you start down the steps, slowly, looking only at me."

No hardship there.

"I'll be coming up. When you're on the step above me, just do what comes naturally. Then they'll stop the camera and have us change positions. Don't worry, don't be nervous, but...we have to get this right. We only have the stairway for a certain length of time, and since you were late, we're cutting it close."

Her eyes widened. Horror must have shown in them because he took her hand and raised it to his lips. "There's no need to worry. You're beautiful, the dress is beautiful. You walk down steps all the time, right?"

"Right," she murmured.

"Anytime, people," Ben called.

"Go on. It'll be fine." Kailen gave her a nudge.

There wasn't anything to do but turn, lift the hem free of her feet, and march up the steps before the little guy, Ben, had a heart attack. She'd try to straighten the mess out later. Besides, as soon as the camera started, they'd know for sure they had the wrong person because she hadn't a *clue* what to do. What would happen then, she didn't want to know.

"Fine, fine. Don't go all the way to the top." It was Ben yelling at her again. Her head began to ache. She wanted nothing more than to yell back at him, but something kept her from it.

She turned, seeing the full picture for the first time. Below her were four cameras, all aimed at the stairway from various angles. Dozens of people milled about inside the roped off area, and many more lingered outside the rope, watching. Ben stood to the left of the stairs with a clear view of all action. She looked down at them and silence descended over the crowd, as though they waited to hear what proclamation she might make. All eyes were on her.

Someone adjusted the spotlight to highlight her, and she squinted then raised her hand to shield her eyes. Even from halfway up the staircase she heard a collective "Ooo," from the people below. One glance down told the story. Bugle beads, seed pearls, sequins glistened and sparkled in the light. With the slightest movement, color swirled from waist to hem. It was remarkable.

It was magical. It was—

"Action!"

Distracted as she was with the way her gown responded to the lighting, she didn't hear Ben.

"Cut!"

"Derica!" Kailen's call was sharp and penetrated her mind.

She looked up from the dress and down to his amused face.

Kailen cocked his head toward Ben who had moved close in and now gazed at her in disgust. "He called action."

"Oh!" She looked at Ben. "Oh, dear. I'm sorry, but the dress...."

She heard Kailen's rich rumble of laughter. "Now you see why it's one of a kind. You can't mass-produce that kind of effect."

"People, do you mind?" Impatience rang in Ben's loud voice. Then his tone softened, but with sarcasm, not real concern. "Are you *ready*, lady?"

She nodded. Glancing at the foot of the stairs and beyond Kailen, she found the lights blinded her to the crowd. Good. That should make this easier. Ben had moved out of her vision. All she could see was Kailen.

"Action!"

With one hand on the balustrade, she stepped down. Kailen stepped up. His eyes focused on hers, willing her to see only him. She couldn't have looked away if she'd wanted to. Like a laser beam he guided her to him, their movements unfailingly matched, until she stood one step above him. For a moment they gazed into each other's eyes. Then he reached around to cup her buttocks and pull her toward him as he leaned into her, resting his head on her breast.

He'd said to do what came naturally. She slid her fingers through his hair to hold his head with one hand. Her other hand rested on his shoulder blades as she bent to kiss the top of his head.

"Cut! Perfect!" The spotlights went out.

They didn't move. Derica felt the hard bulge of his penis against her leg and his hand softly kneaded her butt. He felt so warm, so right standing there against her.

Finally, he pulled away, looking up at her as he moved back. His eyes were dark and hooded. If they'd been alone, she thought he would kiss her, but the noise from the crowd below reminded her that they weren't by themselves.

"He's right, you were perfect."

"I mussed your hair." Her voice was hushed, befitting the scene they'd played more than the reality.

"You did exactly as you should have."

Suddenly they were surrounded by people. Samantha charged up the stairs to check her makeup and hair, and to fix the damage she'd done to Kailen's hair by running her hand through it. Within minutes they were drawn to the base of the stairway.

Kailen leaned close to her to describe the next shoot. "You're to stand here, looking impatient, as though you're waiting for someone."

"That'll be you," she said with a smile.

"Yes," he said, returning the smile and making her heart thump strongly. "I'll come down the steps and behind you. Just follow my lead after that." He turned to move to the other side of the stairs, then stopped. "Are you sure you haven't done this before?"

"Quite sure."

"Well, you're a quick study. It feels right with you. More than right."

More than right. It was perfect. If the ad made women feel the way she felt right now—giddy with desire—it would sell one hell of a lot of perfume, books, whatever.

Kailen walked off as Ben called, "Places!"

The lights came on and she had to keep from shutting her eyes.

"Action!"

Trying to look slightly annoyed, she peered out to where the lobby would be, then rested her hand on the curved end of the balustrade and tapped her fingers. She sensed him before he wrapped his arms around her waist and pulled her tightly against him. His breath was hot as his lips nipped her ear. With the tip of his tongue he traced a path from her ear lobe to her neck. She tilted her head to allow him access, closing her eyes at the sensation. He nibbled, then licked the spot. His hands rose from her waist to the bottom of her breasts, as though any second he would caress them. Derica covered one of his hands with her own, and reached her other hand behind to clasp his leg.

Again she forgot they were in a crowded hotel lobby. With the incredible heat raging between them, it felt as though they were the only people in all the world.

"Cut!"

The lights went out but Kailen didn't release her.

"Another perfect print." Ben stood before her when she forced her eyes open and dropped her hands to her side.

She thought it was with equal reluctance that Kailen moved away, although he kept one arm at her waist.

"We might finish on time after all if you two keep this up. You doing okay, lady?"

"Yes, I'm fine."

"Okay. Kailen." Ben directed his attention to Kailen as Samantha fluttered around them touching up cosmetics, and smoothing hair and skirts alike. "Just three more scenes and we can wrap things up. Keep helping her"—he nodded to Derica—"and it'll go fast. You two are on fire. I think we've got a winner; Violet Passion is supposed to make people feel sex and wild emotion. If I didn't know this was a staged set, I'd think you were ready to hop into bed with each other." He slapped Kailen on the shoulder and hustled away.

"I am," Kailen murmured, slanting a glance at Derica.

For the next forty minutes they performed different scenes, each more intimate than the previous. In the last, she rushed down the stairs and into his arms. His lips crushed to hers, his hand held her tightly against his erection, until he allowed her to slide down his body to the floor. The crew and audience broke into applause when Ben called a wrap.

Kailen lifted his head, separating their lips by a fraction. Slowly, unwillingly, she forced herself to pull away. Never had she felt such animal attraction for any man. It was exhilarating. Her blood was hot, her heart pounded. It was dangerous. This man with the roughened, dark jaw and dazzling diamond in his ear was not the type of man she normally dated, not the kind who fit into the profile as "acceptable" for her career.

Still, she wanted him like she'd wanted no one else. And judging by the glint in his eyes, he wanted her, too.

"What are you doing for the rest of the night?" His voice was husky, sounding as heavy with desire as she felt.

"I have to do what I came here to do. My company is hosting a party."

People moved around them, disconnecting lights and breaking down camera set-ups. For the first time all evening, no one came to make sure her make-up was perfect or each strand of hair was in place.

"So, you really aren't a model, hmm? You're late for your party. Is someone there waiting for you?"

"No one's waiting. Would you like to come with me?" As soon as the words left her mouth she wondered why she'd spoken them. Hadn't she just admitted that he wasn't like the men she dated? That he was dangerous to her career? Too late. His smile said it all.

"I don't want to let you go, so yes, I'll accept your offer."

She tried to backpedal. "I shouldn't have said that—I'm sure you have more exciting things to do. These things are boring even for me. I don't have a choice, but you do. Don't feel obligated."

"I'm not obligated. I want to be with you." He took her arm and guided her away from the crowd. "I do have a question, though."

Derica gratefully retrieved her evening bag from Samantha who had confiscated it when she first arrived, then preceded Kailen to the elevators. He stayed close, not giving her a chance to slip away. Although she was nervous, she also felt energized.

Already the evening had been totally different than she'd thought it would be when she left home. She'd been creative, praised for her work and acclaimed as a beauty. An exciting and handsome man wanted to spend the remainder of the evening with her. *Deri* thought she hadn't been this jazzed in years—for the first time in a long time the party tonight would not be dull. *Derica* worried that damage control might be in order. But neither persona gave a thought to telling Kailen she'd changed her mind.

She pushed the Up button. "What's your question?" she asked, not looking into his face.

"If you weren't sent by the modeling agency, how did you end up with a dress just like 'the' dress?"

"Obviously someone is pulling the wool over your sponsor's eyes. It can't be one of a kind, can it? I'm renting it from a little shop down on Post, so heaven only knows how many copies there must be out there."

Now she did look up, almost losing herself in the depths of his blue, blue eyes. "Or else, it's magic."

Your Desire

Chapter Three

They'd been here a couple of hours already. Half an hour would have been enough for Kailen, but he understood business and knew that Derica had a responsibility to mix and mingle. He'd stayed by her side at first, braving the stares of admiration from the women and those of envy from the men. He was used to the former—no need to profess false modesty. His looks *were* exceptional, and he used them to get everything he could in modeling, in order to support the profession of his heart, painting. As to the latter, he didn't blame the men at all. If someone else had walked in with Derica on his arm, Kailen would have been envious as hell.

After sharing a drink with the owners of MiBar Medical, Mike Hawkins and his wife, Barbara, Kailen had moved around the room on his own. Introducing himself, he'd join in a conversation for a few minutes then move on to another group, all the while keeping his eye on Derica.

The gown was fantastic. It shimmered with every movement, reflecting light in a million directions and seeming to flow with color even when she stood still. She looked regal in that gown, like a queen and like something else, too. Like a Siren. Seductive, dangerous. Sexy as hell. Every time he looked up to find her staring at him, he felt her allure as surely as ancient mariners had felt the Siren's call. If he wasn't careful, he'd find himself crashed on the rocks of Derica Meadows, unable to get away. And that wasn't his style at all.

True, he wanted nothing more than to sink himself into her hot body and fuck her until neither of them knew which end was up, but he also wanted no commitments. If he didn't think he could walk away afterwards, the sex shouldn't happen. Right now, he felt the war between logic and hormones. Whenever it came down to a contest of the two brains, if there was a hint of doubt about what he was jumping into, the big one resting on his shoulders was the usual victor. It's how he'd lived to the ripe old age of thirty-six with no wife and no paternal responsibilities. The way things were with Derica, with the spark she'd lighted in his gut as soon as their eyes met—not to mention the way his cock had come alive since their first touch—he half hoped the little brain would win out, regardless that common sense dictated he take her home and forget her.

"Have you known our Derica long?" A tall, older man holding a tumbler half full of whisky moved into place beside Kailen.

His speech was clear but the redness surrounding his irises indicated the drink he held was far from his first. As bloodshot as his eyes were, his focus centered on Derica, standing halfway across the room with two women who appeared to be giving her a lecture. Their faces were stern and they took turns speaking. Her face held a pleasant look, but vacant, as though her mind were somewhere else. She nodded at regular intervals, but said nothing.

"No, not long."

"God, she looks beautiful tonight." The man pointed in her direction with his glass. "That's why those bitches are giving her hell."

"They're complaining because she looks good?" That didn't make sense to Kailen. But then nothing about this party made sense to him. Gatherings like this were one reason he didn't miss the corporate existence. Just being this close gave him shivers remembering how hard he'd tried to conform to this world, and how he simply couldn't.

"She does look good, doesn't she? Good enough to eat, and I'd try if I thought she'd give me the time of day. Even in those God-awful black things she usually wears to these boring damn parties, most any guy attending would willingly die to fuck her if she gave him the wink and nod. Not that she ever does. Tonight she looks like an angel of sin, and I can tell you there're a lot of hard-ons in the room because of it. Mine included. And *that's* really why those bitches are giving her a hard time."

"Derica seems to be handling it well. How do you know that's what they're doing?"

The man snorted. "Derica is too ambitious for her own good sometimes, so she'll take what they hand out and smile about it. Corporate wives carry a lot of influence in ways no MBA program teaches. And how do I know what they're doing? Because the bitch on the right is my wife. I'll be fucking her tonight for relief, but I won't be thinking about her and she knows it." He emptied his glass and put it on the table behind them. "Now, I'll go and break up the hen party, and you rescue Derica, right?"

Kailen nodded. "Right."

The two men joined the small group. The older women stopped talking as soon as they arrived. One of them stepped possessively closer to Kailen's companion and grasped his arm. He didn't even try to hide his look of displeasure.

Derica looked at the man. "Daniel, I see you've met my friend, Kailen…?"

"Just Kailen," he said, turning to the man.

"We haven't met formally," Daniel replied, and shook Kailen's hand.

"Daniel McNaught is my boss. This is his wife, Hannah, and Victoria, Dr. Haber's wife. We spoke with him shortly after we arrived."

Kailen nodded to the women. They smiled at him, all trace of malice erased from their faces.

"You came with Derica, Kailen?" Victoria asked in a purring voice.

Kailen thought she wasn't bad-looking now, but she must have been a real beauty in her younger days. She spoiled the illusion of pleasantness with her next words, however.

"Wher*ever* did someone like Derica find *you*?"

Daniel raised his brows with a look that said *See? Didn't I tell you they were bitches?*

Kailen wrapped his arm around Derica's waist and pulled her close, an action she mimicked by putting her arm around his waist. "Actually, we just happened into each other earlier tonight, victims of circumstance." He smiled at her. "But after our first kiss, I knew I didn't want to let her go. So, when she invited me to your party, there was no question but that I'd come with her."

"And I'm glad you did," she answered.

"Kailen is such an unusual name," Hannah commented. Her voice grated on his ears.

"It's my stage name." He smiled brilliantly at the women, and they appeared mesmerized. "I do some modeling."

"I knew I'd seen you before!" Victoria looked pleased with herself. "You're on billboards all over town."

"Oh, yes," Hannah said, "for that cologne. Do you do any others?

"None that you'd recognize my face in," he said. He winked at Hannah, and Victoria sucked in a breath.

"You do that ad for the—" Hannah looked at him with widened eyes and gave a surprised, *Oh!* Rather than shock, her eyes held a melting, dreamy gaze.

Derica looked up questioningly, as though trying to place him with something she might have seen around town. "I'm sorry. I don't pay much attention to billboards when I'm driving into work."

"It's a campaign for briefs." He leaned to whisper in her ear, knowing the two women were watching every move. "Maybe later tonight you'll get a view that'll bring the ad to mind." He was delighted to see her eyes darken as a smile played across her lips.

"I hope you'll be coming to more company functions, Kailen," Victoria said, a smile in her voice. She stepped forward and smoothed her hand along his forearm.

"Thank you, *Mrs.* Haber. Maybe Derica will invite me." At his emphasis on her married name, Victoria's face creased with a frown.

"I think I heard your husband asking where you were, Victoria. And I'm sure Derica and Kailen would like to dance or have some time to themselves?" Daniel directed the question to Kailen.

"Yes," Kailen agreed, watching Derica. "Let's dance a little before I take you home."

They seemed to glide to the dance floor. Taking her in his arms and moving to the melody played by the band felt wonderful, but keeping in mind where they were, he didn't pull her close like he wanted to.

"Are they always this self-absorbed?" His voice was pitched low.

"This, and worse. Isn't it amazing? I admit to having had a good time watching the women trip all over themselves getting to meet you, though. And seeing their expressions when they realized you were with me."

"Why would they be surprised we were together?"

"In case you didn't realize it, you're classified as a full-fledged hunk. They see me as a simple, dull accountant." She drew her head back and stared at him. "Don't tell me you didn't get a wad of phone numbers."

He chuckled. "I did." He kissed her forehead. "But of all the women here, I'd pick you. I *do* pick you. And you might be surprised—these women don't think you're a simple, dull accountant. Know why? Because 'simple' is the last word that comes to the men's minds when they think of you. In fact, the impression I got tonight is that men don't *use* their minds too much when they look at you. Certainly not tonight, in that dress and with the glow about you. You can trust me on that."

She sighed. "Too much drinking."

"Not at all." Then he gave in to what he wanted and tightened his hold.

Even through the material of his tux and her dress, their bodies molded to each other perfectly. With only short steps left and right, barely moving them at all, he managed to rub against her, bringing him torturous bliss.

He dropped his head to whisper in her ear. "Do you know what you've been doing to me all night? I look at you and can't catch my breath. You smile and my blood pounds, racing to one location. Can you guess where that is?" He tasted her lobe.

"I have some idea." Thrusting her hips forward, she chuckled at his groan.

"We shouldn't take this any further here," he said in a quiet voice that rasped with desire. "Can you leave?"

"I'll die if we stay any longer. But…" She hesitated, but then forged on. "Maybe we could get something to eat on the way out. These events always make me hungry and I don't like to eat much while I'm here."

He raised his head to brush his lips across hers, then grabbed her hand and tugged her to the exit. In minutes they were on the street, walking toward the corner and a well-known deli. As they passed a trash can, Kailen stopped and withdrew papers and napkins from his jacket pocket. He dropped the stack of phone numbers into the trash, then wrapped Derica's hand more firmly in his as they walked on.

*

The deli had proven not only to be packed but to have a decibel level above what OSHA would recommend for a factory. "Do you want to wait for a table?" he'd practically yelled at her.

She'd shaken her head and they pushed their way back out onto the sidewalk. With some reluctance at first, she'd suggested another place to get a sandwich. "The selection is limited, but it's quiet and the service is good."

"Where is that?" he'd asked.

"My place. I hesitate because I don't know you. I don't normally take strangers home."

"We've been with each other for hours, so I'm not a total stranger, and this night has hardly been normal, has it?"

His argument had convinced her, and now here they were, entering a small but nice apartment off Lombard.

The first thing that struck him when he entered was its neatness. Nothing looked out of place. Derica excused herself to change clothes, and he walked around the living room examining the books filling the shelves against one wall, the music CDs neatly arranged in order by artist, the trade magazines fanned out on the coffee table. He had a perverse desire to rearrange them so that Accounting Today came after Business Practices. Or worse, to toss the perfectly spaced pillows on the sofa onto the floor.

Smiling to himself, he pulled off his tie and removed the first three studs from his shirt. He laid his jacket along the back of the sofa and took off his shoes. Giving a sigh of relief, he leaned his head back, closed his eyes and propped his feet on the coffee table, flexing his toes in pleasure.

"You look comfortable," Derica said.

His eyes popped open, then he sat up and gave her a full, appreciative look. A loose skirt almost reached her knees, hanging low on her hips where the hem of a tee shirt met the waistband. The slightest movement of her arms exposed an inch or two of bare midriff. The tight nubs of her breasts poked the tee shirt, leaving no question that her bra had been left in the bedroom.

In a flash his groin tightened.

"Want some music while we eat?" She sounded nervous. Looked nervous, too, breathing fast and clenching her hands in front of her, as she watched him gaze at her. His hunger must have been evident on his face, and it wasn't for ham and Swiss.

"Sure," he said casually, "music is good."

She made her way behind the sofa to the stereo and CDs, but she couldn't have been prepared for his lightning movements when he grabbed her waist, twisted on the sofa and dragged her over the back. Her exclamation of surprise was swallowed by his lips on hers as he settled her on his lap.

In seconds, her surprise turned to whimpers of need. Her hands tangled in his hair and her mouth opened. He rearranged her more comfortably over his erection before reaching under her tee. His tongue explored her mouth. She tasted minty, and must have brushed her teeth when she went to change clothes.

Her breasts weren't large but they were soft he discovered, as his hand caressed her. Lightly he kneaded each globe of flesh, then pinched her nipples until she moaned. He broke the kiss and leaned Derica back against the arm of the sofa. He moved down, placing one of her legs on the floor. Raising her shirt, he bent his head to take her breast in his mouth, while kneading the other with his hand.

"Yes," she whispered. "Yes."

He licked a path from one breast to the other, and moved his hand down her body to the hem of her skirt. Spears of anticipation stabbed him as he ran his hand along the supple skin of her thigh. Then he stopped. No panties. He raised his head to look at her face.

She opened her eyes to stare back. Brazenly, without saying a word, she moved her leg on the floor, spreading herself wide for him.

"You're a wonder, Derica."

She smiled. Such a smile! Even in the midst of seduction, his mind imagined painting her wearing that smile and nothing else. The composition formed in his mind in a heartbeat. But after tonight he would probably never see her again. If the party and the world in which she worked hadn't told him, her apartment did. They might have been similar at one time, but now they were from two different ways of life. At this point, things would never work between them. Too bad, because she was beautiful, sensuous, and seemed to match him desire for desire.

He bent to lave her nipple with his tongue then suckle each breast. His fingers trailed through her soft pubic curls before dipping past the folds of her labia and into her slick channel.

"You're so wet," he said against her breast. With a final lick over her nipple, he watched her reaction to his attention.

Two fingers easily slid in and out of her pussy. He pressed three together and gave her the friction she would need to come. Allowing his thumb to glide over her clit as his fingers fucked her, he heard her moan.

Reaching up, she grasped the arm of the sofa, pulling on it to fill the need to hold something. Her mouth fell open; her eyes shut more tightly. Her hips rose and fell against his hand.

"Oh! Oh, oh, *oh*!"

Her vaginal muscles clamped his fingers. Convulse, relax, convulse, relax. If it had been his cock inside her, he wouldn't have been able to resist coming, not with her muscles so strongly milking him. *Damn!* He wanted his cock inside her.

She gasped for air, then began to calm. He pulled his fingers out, dripping wet with her juices. Her eyes slowly opened, her cheeks rosy with the effects of her release.

He licked his index finger then sucked it. Her eyes were unbelievably wide, watching him. Deliberately, he held his middle finger to her lips. She opened and he slid it in. Sucking, she produced the same milking effect her pussy had moments before.

Pulling his finger back, he smiled at her. Kailen was hard as a rock, but he was willing to prolong the night. "Did you say something about sandwiches?"

Derica returned his smile. "I did. Want to come into the kitchen, and we'll fix something to help us get through the rest of the night?"

"I have a feeling we'll need it," he said, and helped her up.

* * * *

Who in the world was this man, and how did she end up with him here in her home, where only a few men had ever been as her lover? She was always so sensible. Until tonight she'd never done anything to stray from the accepted path for her career. Or at least she hadn't flaunted it. Kailen wasn't on that path. Kailen wasn't even someone she knew, yet she'd brought him here, to her place. A shiver of apprehension ran down her spine.

A tingle of excitement followed close behind. Watching him now, spreading mayonnaise on bread before layering shaved turkey and ham over the cheese already there, it was almost impossible to imagine he'd had three fingers inside her only a few minutes ago, bringing her to climax in a glorious burst of color and stars behind the closed lids of her eyes. If not for the relaxed, sated contentment radiating through her body, she might think she'd made up the experience.

Kailen didn't look as though anything out of the ordinary had happened. Head bent, he concentrated on creating his meal. She poured two glasses of Chardonnay and nibbled on chips.

Suddenly, he raised his eyes to her. Dark as the midnight heaven and twice as deep, they pierced straight to her heart. She took a breath at the raw hunger she saw and knew in that moment he was no more untouched by their encounter in the living room than she.

"Aren't you hungry?" he asked.

"Very." She couldn't keep heat from flooding her cheeks. Although she was no virginal schoolgirl—far from it, in fact—it had been a long dry spell since her last lover.

"I am, too. I've always had a strong appetite." He glanced to the place in front of her, empty of food. "Maybe you'd like to eat some of what I have."

She licked her lips. This flirtatious, sexual innuendo was powerful foreplay. "I'm sure what you have is great. I can almost taste it already."

Even his chuckle was seductive, skimming along her nerves, bringing every bit of her to life. Without looking down, she knew her nipples stood at attention, tenting her tee shirt. Her thighs were damp with freshly flowing juices. His nostrils flared, and she knew the scent of her arousal filled him.

Focusing once more on the sandwich, Kailen sliced it, handing Derica half. He raised one of the glasses in a toast. "To voracious appetites."

She smiled and clinked her glass against his.

"And more importantly, to satisfying them." Holding her gaze, he took a sip then set the glass on the table.

"Oh my God, I don't think I can wait much longer."

He laughed. "Patience. I'll do my best to make it worth your while." Then, as though nothing had passed between them, he took a bite.

She fell into a chair and took a bite, too, followed with a sip of wine. She was so hot. If her apartment had air conditioning, she'd have it on, set low.

"So, you're an accountant." He grinned at her after taking a drink. "And a sometimes model."

She snorted. "A no-times model. Wait until the agency hears what happened. That poor girl, Madeline or whatever her name is. I just hope I didn't screw things up." Appreciation filled her that he was trying to make the moment feel normal. Forcing herself to focus on conversation, she finally tamed the blazing fire burning to have him deep inside her.

"You were perfect. We have chemistry and it'll show through. This campaign is going to be dynamite."

"Well, you know your stuff. I couldn't have moved without your help tonight. Thanks." Another sip of wine, another bite of sandwich. She put the food aside and moved the wine glass in front of her. "Do you get a lot of modeling jobs?"

Pressing her legs tightly together, she tried not to think of the wetness even now marking her skirt. Ask a question, listen to the answer. Conversation is easy, right? *Hell no.*

He shrugged and put the last piece of bread in his mouth. "A fair number. I'm also a courier."

"Courier? One of those guys on bikes all over the city?" Surprise forced her mind off of her need. At last.

Nodding, he said, "Yeah, that's me. Keeps me in shape." He winked. "Are you going to eat the rest of your sandwich?"

Handing it to him, she watched as he finished eating. "So you're a courier and a model."

"And a painter. A few days a month at this, a few days at that. I do everything part time. Except painting—that occupies my heart and soul full time."

"An artist! What do you paint?"

"Masterpieces," he quipped.

She smiled.

"Actually, I started years ago creating custom canvases for designers in town. The work I do for myself is slightly…edgier, different." Kailen cast her a look as though to gauge her reaction.

"Different how?" Leaning forward, she found herself fascinated by this man of multiple talents.

He grinned. "I have a show in a few weeks. Maybe you'll come. Then you can tell *me* how they're different." With one quick gulp he emptied his glass and stood. "As neat as your apartment is, I know you don't leave dishes on the table, so let's clean up then we'll see about dessert."

Dessert? Quickly she ran through a mental inventory of what she had on hand that comprised dessert and came up wanting. *And speaking of wanting…* She didn't want dessert, damn it, she wanted him.

With so little to put away, it took no time before the kitchen looked the way it had before they'd eaten. She draped the dishrag over the faucet and dried her hands. Kailen wrapped his arms around her waist and nibbled her neck before turning her around.

"Hmm, dessert," he murmured.

"I'm afraid I don't have anything."

"Baby, you've got it all." Examining her face, he quirked a smile. "Don't tell me you've forgotten our appetizer. I'm ready for another course now." His mouth descended to cover hers as his hands slid under her shirt.

She raised her arms. He lifted his head only long enough to peel off her tee. Soft and pliant, his lips smoothed, then coaxed hers apart. His tongue invaded her mouth, hot and demanding, to meet hers. Hiking her skirt to her waist, his hands massaged her bare butt, squeezing her cheeks and running his fingers along the cleft separating them.

Heat built deep inside, melting in a pool between her legs. She wanted him more than she'd ever wanted another man. If he didn't do something about it soon, she'd have to take matters into her own hands. Assertive at work, she'd always let the man be the aggressor in lovemaking. But since meeting Kailen, she'd felt compelled to act outside her normal behavior. He'd been right when he said nothing about this night had been commonplace. Nothing about this man was, either.

Frantic for relief, she tilted her head for better access and thrust her tongue into his mouth. His grunt of approval drove her further. Grasping at his shirt, she jerked it from the waistband of his trousers, then fumbled with the zipper. Finally, she was able to drag his pants over his hips and down his thighs.

Panting with desire, she shoved him away to gain room to drop to her knees. He said nothing, but the roughness of his breathing told her all she needed to know about how affected he was by their love play. Eschewing finesse, she eased his briefs over his erection then yanked briefs and pants to his ankles. He stepped out of them and she brushed them aside.

Hard and thick, like a compass pointing due north, his cock aimed unerringly for her mouth. She took a second or two to admire the mass of dark curly hair at the base of his penis and the heaviness of his balls, before circling the smooth purple knob of his cock with her tongue.

"Oh, God, baby, yes." His hands guided her head to meet the gentle thrust of his hips, sliding himself into her mouth.

She didn't give head often. Had refused to, in fact, on more than one occasion, but she relished taking Kailen to her throat. Her lips clamped around him as she moved forward and back, slipping him in and out. With each stroke, her tongue caressed his length. Steadying herself with one hand on his hip, she used the other to fondle the heavy sac that tapped her throat on each downward sweep.

His flavor was wonderful, his scent intoxicating. The size of his cock filled her mouth, stretching her lips almost to the point of pain. Would he stretch her pussy like that, too? With a frenzy she'd hardly felt before, every nerve in her body screamed to find out.

She felt his scrotum tighten, and Kailen tugged her head away. She looked up. His eyes appeared slightly glazed and his mouth hung open, but his lips turned up in a smile.

"Come up here. It's my turn." He helped her stand. "I like to eat my dessert on the table." Lifting her easily, he used his foot to push the chair aside so he could set her on the edge of the Formica dinette. He pulled her skirt to her waist.

One big hand pressed her back onto the table, the other spread her legs. "Look at this," he said, running his finger through the folds of her labia, "you're almost dripping, you're so wet. And you smell so great. This is my treat."

Using his hands to hold her legs apart, he dipped his head to her, allowing his tongue to brush from clit to vagina and back again, over and over.

Derica moaned. His tongue left trails of fire. She wanted his control, his heat. Needed for him do whatever it took to bring her relief from the ache he'd started. As though she'd spoken aloud, he focused his glorious tongue on her clit, licking, encircling the swollen nub until it throbbed. At the same time, his fingers slid in and out of her pussy. It took no time for her to come, trembling with the effort and whimpering with the aftershocks.

He left her for a few moments. When she forced her eyes open, he was once again standing between her legs, lifting them to his shoulders, and pulling her to the edge.

"Here we go, baby." The head of his penis poised to invade her opening, still throbbing and wet from her orgasm. He pushed gently, easily gaining access, but allowing her body time to adjust to his size and need. She required it. Even the lubrication from her climax wasn't enough to fully prepare her for his size.

"You're so tight. God, it feels good." Grasping her hips for leverage, he began a steady push and pull.

With each movement he rubbed her clit. She thought she'd die from the exquisite pleasure, and she didn't mind the thought.

"You're beautiful, Derica. Not just your natural beauty, but the way you look spread here for me. No embarrassment, no holding back your sensuality. You give as good as you get."

Languidly, her eyes opened to gaze at him. She saw her ankles around his neck, and the movement of his hips increasing their tempo as he spoke. His voice was raspy. The hold he maintained on her hips was almost painful, but she didn't care. Her breath came in gasps as she rocked on the tabletop.

"Your tits are red where I sucked them earlier, and your lips are swollen and look well-used from when you sucked me. The sight of me in your mouth almost made me come. Would you have taken me?"

"Yes."

He shut his eyes. His strokes were long and hard.

She couldn't hold any longer, and felt herself break apart, a million stars falling through a black universe. The only sound in the room was her groan of release—or was it Kailen's? Did he stop moving? All she knew or cared about was the pulsating sensation radiating throughout her body from her core. It seemed never to end.

When she became aware of her surroundings, her legs dangled off the table and Kailen lay over her, his head nestled between her breasts. She brought her hand up to stroke his hair.

"Are you all right?" he asked.

"Better than all right."

With some effort, he pushed himself up, then helped her sit. She hadn't given it a moment's thought, but her mind was eased when she saw the condom covering his penis, the tip filled with cum. When she looked up, she saw his smile.

"Appetizer, entrée and dessert. What's next?"

She slid to the floor and took his hand. Starting for the bedroom she said, "Sleep, interrupted by a few snacks."

He laughed. "I love a woman who enjoys eating."

Chapter Four

Hot and cold. Burning with desire to feel his hands on her again, freezing from the rebuff he'd dealt by leaving her bed Sunday morning without a word. Derica alternated between the two extremes all week.

When she'd awoken naked and alone, she stretched, reveling in the aches that signaled dormant muscles recently used. And how deliciously they'd been used! She smiled, even as her hands smoothed across bruises where Kailen's fingers or mouth had left their marks in the midst of passion. Never had she known a man to be so inventive in his lovemaking, or so excited over her attentions to him. He seemed to enjoy every aspect of the physical to the fullest extent. She'd sensed it from the first in him, but was stunned to discover it in herself.

Kailen was the most wrong man ever for her. Absolutely *wrong*. But she wanted him, all of him. It was a like a blazing, living fire, the need she felt, and it would consume her if he didn't come to her soon.

She'd gone in search of him but the apartment had been empty of his existence except for the several used condoms in her bathroom trash can.

Frantically, she'd dressed and raced from the building. The sidewalks were empty, but she ran to Powell Street anyway, feeling the need for some action even if it was useless. To the left, the Bay was shrouded in fog. From the right, the morning bells pealed from the cathedral, calling worshippers to Mass. As she feared would be the case, Kailen was nowhere to be seen.

Returning to the apartment, she'd searched for a note but found nothing. The day ahead had suddenly seemed empty. She filled it with laundry and rationalizing all of the reasons why his going was for the best.

It had been a night of fantasy, with no promises asked or made. They were too different for anything long-lasting. He didn't fit the ideal of a man she should be with. Certainly his choice of profession—professions, considering he modeled, delivered letters, and painted "edgy" pictures—wasn't desirable. In addition, he was too out of the mainstream to be part of her colleagues' lifestyle. A lifestyle she not only aspired to herself, but needed to fit in order to succeed in *her* chosen profession.

Yes, definitely, his exit from her life was the best thing. She repeated that sentiment all morning as she washed clothes, but it felt just as wrong the hundredth time as it had the first.

Logically it made sense, but logic couldn't stop her from craving him. It wasn't just the sex, although the sex had been incredible, fantastic, worth killing for. It wasn't his witty conversation or intriguing hints about his lifestyle. It wasn't even the way he made her feel like she was the only woman in the world when he looked at her. It was…well, it was all of it.

Tossing a blouse on the bed unfolded, she'd grabbed the phone book and searched not only for his name but for any art gallery that might advertise his work. She'd never realized how many galleries there were in San Francisco. It would take days to query them all for a clue of how to find him.

On Monday morning, she'd received a call from Ben's office. The film director's secretary asked her to come downtown to sign the rest of the paperwork for the Violet Passion ad, and to straighten matters out with the agency, which didn't understand how the mix-up had occurred. However, the young woman said that considering how well the shoot had gone, the agency's representative would be interested in talking to her about a contract.

Derica suddenly realized she held all the cards. "I'll sign the papers to release my work on the ad if you give me Kailen's name and address."

The secretary refused, citing privacy.

"Please look carefully at the papers you hold. I filled in the contact information, not the release information. I knew there had been a mistake, even if no one would listen to me. If Ben wants the work he did Saturday night to stand, I want the information about Kailen."

The woman mumbled something about how she'd have no time for work if she gave Kailen's number out to every woman who asked for it, then she asked Derica to hold. Half a minute later, Ben came on the line.

"Miss Meadows, it was so nice working with you Saturday. When can you stop by to sign the paperwork to release what we did? I've already seen the preliminary prints, and they're fabulous." Was this the same man who had screamed at her across the lobby of downtown's most prestigious hotel? His tone was so conciliatory, so soft, so…. She could almost feel Ben's lips on her right rear cheek, next to where Kailen had actually kissed her.

The thought of Kailen's mouth on her butt sent her heart into overdrive, and reminded her of her mission. "Ben, it's very nice of you to say that. I'm glad the work turned out well, and I'm sure you wouldn't want to have to repeat the process. Now, did your secretary tell you what I need?"

"Yes, she did. Now Miss… Do you mind if I call you Derica?"

She hummed.

"Good. Derica, you know we can't do that. You wouldn't want me to give out your name and address, would you?"

"Of course not. I'd sue you all the way to next Sunday if you did."

"So you see why—"

"No release without his name and address. Phone number, too, just to be safe."

There was silence, then, "Just a minute." The obsequiousness was gone.

Flipping through papers on her desk as she waited, she was surprised at how quickly Ben came back on the line.

"You can pick up the information you're looking for when you come in to sign the papers, Derica. Once everything is tied up, I think we'll both be happy."

She had gone that very afternoon, during lunch. Making it clear to the agency rep with whom she spoke that she wasn't interested in a modeling career, she'd assigned a charity to receive all of her proceeds from the ad. After signing the appropriate X-marked lines, she'd casually accepted the sheet of notebook paper Ben's secretary handed her and left the glamorous life of modeling behind her.

Once on the street, she'd whipped the folded paper open. *Steven Hooper.* Ordinary enough for a courier, but not sufficient for a master of sensual delight. No, Kailen suited that persona far better.

Below his name was the address for a building of live/work lofts off the Embarcadero, and a phone number. She'd calmly put the paper in her desk drawer when she returned to the office, and there it had stayed, all week, calling to her. As impossible to ignore as a ringing phone or crying baby, it had taken discipline each day not to leave work and run to his place. But she hadn't. Instead, she'd waited to see if he would call her.

At first, she was certain he would. She couldn't have been alone in her desire, could she? Surely he couldn't have faked the way his breath hitched when she tongued him or the moans that changed to cries of triumph when he came. The intensity with which he'd loved her—didn't it mean something special to him, too? Or was she being something she'd never been in her life—a silly female—expecting Kailen to feel the same thing for their lovemaking that she did?

Her work week had been fine. A new position was announced and her boss, Daniel, had hinted that she was perfectly positioned for advancement. But each day with no word from Kailen was harder to take. Plagued with thoughts of him doing with other women what he'd done with her, she felt sick. Her appetite left and sleep eluded her. She knew she had to take steps or go crazy.

With a feeling of trepidation that was quite unlike her, she knocked on Kailen's door that Saturday, just before noon. For several moments there was no sound. Then she heard a woman's voice.

Oh, God! There was no way she could face in reality the visions that had tortured her all week. Seeing Kailen with another woman would kill her. She had to escape, and fast.

Before she took five steps the door opened.

"Derica?" It was him. His voice sounded gruff, not welcoming.

She stopped and slowly turned. Filling the doorway, he rested his arm along the top of the frame and cocked his hip against the wall, watching her. He gave no smile, no indication of how he felt about seeing her again. His faded blue jeans topped ragged sneakers, and a sleeveless denim shirt, buttoned up the front, was streaked with paint. His other hand clutched a rag also smeared with various colors.

"Hello, Kailen. I-I wanted to talk with you about the shoot." A lie she hoped he couldn't detect. She'd grasp at any straw to find some logical reason for being outside his doorway, unannounced on a Saturday morning. There was the truth, of course. The conviction that she would die if she didn't make love with him again. But it was better he not know that fact.

Movement behind him drew her eye. A gorgeous woman peeked curiously around his arm. Inky black hair hung to her waist and immense almond-shaped eyes showcased a petite brown face. Derica took a shaky breath and willed herself to calmness. The woman was naked. Sure, a satin robe was draped over her shoulders, but it hung open enough to reveal that there was nothing but skin under it.

"I didn't realize you were busy. I should have called. Sorry." She backed down the hall as she spoke, determined to make good her get away before breaking down.

"You want to talk about the shoot?" His tone, slightly warmer, arrested her backward movement. He said something in a low voice to the woman beside him, and she disappeared. Then he held the door open, stepping back at the same time he extended his hand to her.

Just as when she'd first seen him, she had no alternative but to take it.

He pulled her inside and closed the door. "I'm painting," was all he said. He turned and walked toward the far end of the huge room. She followed.

He pointed to the right. "Kitchen. Help yourself to whatever. I'll be another hour or two."

Looking around curiously as she walked behind him, Derica took in the mismatched furniture littered with books and magazines, clothes and shoes, and the basic jumble that seemed to make up his home. The table in the kitchen showed empty pizza boxes and beer cans, and there were dishes in the sink. Partitioned from sight was what she assumed was his bedroom, since she didn't see a bed anywhere else.

The farthest area of the loft was obviously his studio. It occupied the most space and was the brightest section, with skylights slanted into the roof, supplementing a bank of walled windows. Stacks of canvasses lined one wall, a workbench filled another.

Near the third, positioned to benefit most from the light, was a set or exhibit. Three poles draped in pink chiffon formed a tent. On a sumptuous pallet covered in rose-leaf green colored chiffon and richly braided pillows, lay a young woman. She'd been wrong. There were *two* women here with him, both naked.

The woman on the pallet had each foot tied with a strip of satin to the pole nearest it. Her eyes were covered. The same material secured her hands, which were suspended up and back toward the head pole by the Asian woman Derica had seen from the hall.

Kailen had already resumed his position behind an easel and had paintbrush in hand. "Derica, this is Noelani and Fauve. Fauve can't see you since she's blindfolded, but that won't stop her from making comments about what she thinks you look like. Girls, this is Derica."

"Hello, Derica," the petite Asian-looking woman said with a smile. In one hand she held Fauve's hands aloft. In her other hand she held a peacock feather positioned at Fauve's shaven pussy, as though she were teasing it. The thought made Derica squirm and her groin tighten with anticipation of what the activity would bring.

"Derica, hello. Kailen has told us nothing about you, but I'll bet you're just beautiful, since Kailen only makes time for beautiful women. What do you do? How did you meet?"

The woman who was at the mercy of satin and feather appeared to be gorgeous. She was tall, judging by the length of the pallet she occupied. Her luxuriant red hair waved below the blindfold to her shoulders, and although her form was slender, her breasts were full, tipped with dark pink nipples. "By the way, he's been a bear all week. If you're the reason, we certainly hope you're here to straighten him out."

"Shut up, Fauve," Kailen said, but without heat.

"Yes, master," she answered with a giggle, matched by Noelani's.

He turned to her. "I can't talk now. I only have the right light for a while longer. You want to wait?"

"Oh, yes. Will it bother you if I watch?"

"No." And he faced the easel again, to work.

It was the last he said to her for almost two hours, when he called an end to the day's work. During that time her emotions had run the full gamut. Fear that he'd reject her, primarily, but also hurt that he seemed so cavalier about her visit. As though it was nothing special, nothing that excited him.

When she'd seen the models, jealousy had overwhelmed her. They were beautiful and naked, and claimed all of his attention. But she'd finally seen that Kailen's concentration was for his work, not his models, and gradually she relaxed enough to watch what he was doing. She'd also looked around his studio and discovered that his current work was but one example of what he called "edgy and different." All of his painting was like sex conveyed to canvas.

Now, arching his back and stretching his arms over his head, he looked tired but elated. He helped Noelani untie Fauve, then walked away to care for his brushes. The women stretched and smiled at her as they passed. Proclaiming hunger, they dashed first to the bathroom then the kitchen where she heard them puttering. Kailen seemed uninterested in the fact that two gorgeous, naked women paraded around his home.

Or that she was there. He still hadn't spoken, or even looked her way. Mentally shrugging, she decided to give him a few more minutes before admitting that her presence meant nothing to him.

She took that time to study his work. In the reality of the afternoon light, the women had looked blatantly sexual. In the shading Kailen added, they were softened. The painting was brought to life by the boldness of his strokes and the sharp colors of the tent, the pillows, the greens and blues of the peacock feather, while the women themselves seemed mere impressions, like a dream. Their presence in the work was in no doubt, nor was what they were doing, but the overall effect was the height of sensuality, not sexuality. The work could almost hang in someone's living room, it seemed so refined. Unless one studied it. Then only a boudoir would suit.

Her nipples beaded and her heart rate increased standing in the brightness of the studio. In a different environment, the piece would be an even more powerful aphrodisiac.

"What do you think?" Kailen had arrived behind her without her being aware.

"It's utterly fantastic. Carnal, yet somehow civilized. Civilized, yet decadent. Repeating the pattern of the triangle—the smallest stable figure in nature—and using stroke and color to emphasize the act instead of the people. The smaller figure dominating the larger… It's wonderful on so many levels."

"Yeah, but does it make you hot?" She could hear the grin in his voice.

She turned to face him. "If only you knew."

He leaned down to kiss her. "I want to find out, right now."

It was the strangest feeling, being held against his erection, knowing the rough texture of his hand on her breasts and the silky smoothness of his tongue in her mouth, while hearing the voices of his models wander around the kitchen and living room.

Dropping his head, he took her nipple into his mouth and sucked it through her tee shirt and bra. She arched her back, giving him more.

He straightened, lifting her into his arms, then strode to a door in the partition and pushed it open with his foot. Setting her on the bed, he said, "Get comfortable. I'll be right back."

Derica had pulled her tee shirt off before he left the room. She heard Fauve's and Noelani's feeble protests when Kailen told them to leave, but it didn't take long before the front door closed and there was silence.

Barefoot, he came back with the stealthy grace of a big cat stalking prey. His shirt was gone and his jeans undone when he entered the room. Derica lay naked, propped against the pillows. He stared for only a moment before pushing jeans and briefs to the floor and stepping out of them.

This was what she'd waited for all week. His look, his touch. Open-mouthed kisses that sent her flying, and finally his cock, buried deeply in her. The tension in her belly already gripped her. She couldn't wait, *wouldn't* wait. No foreplay necessary.

She held out her arms.

Starting at the foot of the bed, he crawled toward the head, kissing her ankles, knees, and thighs on his way. When he pushed her legs apart to find her clit and suck it into his mouth, she whimpered.

He looked up and must have sensed her need because he sat on his knees and opened the drawer to the night table. Sheathing himself in the condom took mere seconds, and before she could beg, "Please..." he had slipped inside and initiated her journey to a shattering climax. God, when had she ever come so quickly before?

He lay propped on his elbows, chest to breasts. Her legs, wrapped around his waist, held him tightly to her, but not as tightly as she wanted. Hot breath tickled her ear, and she waited for him to start again.

"What took you so damn long?" His voice rasped in her ear.

So long? Hadn't she climaxed within seconds of his touching her? Her hand felt the muscles in his shoulders bunch. Tension radiated through him everywhere her fingers lit.

"So long to do what?" Turning her head, she kissed his neck, nipped his shoulder with her teeth. Trying to move under him, to begin a rhythm, she found it hard to believe she wanted him again so soon.

What was *wrong* with her? This was alley cat behavior. Fast fucks in the afternoon with a virtual stranger weren't her speed at all. But she loved it with Kailen. He was a drug.

He raised his head to stare into her eyes. His were dangerously dark. "What took you so long to come to me? Ben called Monday to say you wanted my address. Here it is Saturday."

She was astounded. "You *wanted* me to come to you? Well, why didn't you *call*? Why did you leave last week without a word or a note?" Reaching up, she palmed the coarse bristles on his clenched jaw while her thumb traced a path across his cheek.

"I'm not what you need. I'm not good for you, for your career. I know it and you know it, so I guess I should be asking why you're here at all." Seeming to answer the question, his hips pushed forward, pressing into her and rubbing against her sensitive clit.

"Ohhh, God." She brought his mouth to hers and their tongues rubbed and mated until they broke off, gasping for breath.

"Is this the only reason you're here?" He thrust again and she groaned. "Because of what I make you feel when I'm inside you?" And again he moved.

"Yes!"

Fleeting emotions in his expression caused her to stop. For a brief moment, a look of caring had shown in his eyes followed swiftly by disappointment, before his expression became neutral again. She cradled his head in her hands.

"I don't know, Kailen. I just know that for years the most important thing in my life has been my job. This week I couldn't concentrate on work. All I thought about was you, and how much I burned for you. I wanted you to call me. Every time my phone rang, at the office or at home, I prayed it was you telling me you burned, too. By the time the weekend arrived I knew your not calling meant I wasn't important to you, that I was someone you could forget. But I couldn't forget you, not for a minute. I couldn't have gone another day without seeing you."

She leaned up to kiss him, and his expression softened. "Why did you leave me like that last week?"

"Later. Right now let me show you that I *did* burn for you last week. All. Last. Miserable. Damn. Week." He punctuated each word with a hard, deep thrust, sending her over the edge yet again. Then, with his head thrown back and a guttural cry torn from his throat, he followed her.

* * * *

Goddamn! He could barely catch his breath. Her pussy milked his cock like a riptide dragged a swimmer away from the shore. Even through the rubber the sensation was earth-shattering. He could only imagine how it might feel skin to skin. The thought sent a shiver down his back.

It was satisfying to know that Derica was as affected by their sex as he. Her breaths came in fast, soft pants, pushing nipples still firm from her orgasm into his chest. The heel of her right foot lazily rubbed his butt, and her musk filled his nostrils. He wanted her again. If she opened her eyes would he see the same desire reflected there? It was something of a shock to admit that he wanted to.

Bending his head, he licked a drop of sweat from her neck. She groaned, bringing her left foot up to join her right, rubbing, smoothing his ass, pushing him into her. Her arms encircled his neck and she moved her mouth under his, an open, moist invitation for his tongue. He slipped it in, pulled it out. She sucked it back, in the same way her pussy muscles had just pulled on his cock. Incredibly, he hardened again, pushing the full condom up along her thigh as his erection grew.

He broke the kiss to push to his knees. "Gotta get rid of this." He pulled the condom off and dropped it beside the bed then reached for a fresh one.

"Let me," she said, sitting up and taking the packet from him. Fitting it on the head of his penis, she rolled the latex over and down his length. Stroking him between her hands, she leaned forward to suck his nipple at the same time.

Kailen thought he'd pop if she didn't stop. "I'm not going to be able to hold off if you keep it up," he choked out.

"I'm not worried," she said with a throaty chuckle. "Keeping it up is your specialty, I think."

"Get on your hands and knees." He backed off the bed and arranged her at the edge.

Her butt was smooth and milky white. Tempted to do more, he satisfied himself with a sweet kiss on her cheek. She looked over her shoulder at him, then dropped to her elbows, thrusting her ass into the air and wiggling.

He massaged her cheeks, enjoying the feel of the silkiness under his hands. Again, a painting flashed into his mind. Derica, posed just as she was, bare-bottomed but wearing a frilly teddy, lace thigh-highs and heels. He knew in detail how he'd paint that seductive smile and her warm brown eyes alive with the knowledge that soon a cock would invade her pussy. And her expression would whisper that she couldn't wait.

Suddenly, neither could he. He spread her legs and pushed into her, a gentle entry until he was in all the way. He stood still, reveling in the sensation of being buried to the hilt in her heat.

With an audibly deep breath, she dropped her head and pushed back, taking him even deeper than he'd thought possible.

"Yes, baby, yes." Backward and forward. Thrust and draw out, all the time meeting her increasingly faster movements. His balls slapped against her.

He heard her breathing, ragged and shallow. She moaned sharply and came, gripping him, releasing him, as strongly as before. His scrotum drew up, and the spring of tension coiled inside him until he had no choice but to let it go.

"God, yes!" Holding her hips firmly against him he spurted over and over into the condom while lights flashed behind his closed eyelids. He couldn't move. His orgasm seemed to go on and on.

Finally, he had nothing left to release. He felt strangely as though he had nothing left in him at all, and he pulled the rubber off his limp dick. Derica fell to her side, then half pulled, half pushed herself to the head of the bed. He picked up the first condom and dropped them both in the trash can beside the bedside table before collapsing next to her.

"Is that what you came here for, Derica?" He didn't think he had the energy for even a kiss, but somehow he found enough to wrap his arm around her as she snuggled to his side.

She shook her head. "More," she whispered, moments before her breathing turned deep and steady.

"I don't know if more is good for you, but to hell with what's good. More is what I'll try to give you," he murmured into her hair. Then he closed his eyes and drifted into a deeper sleep than he'd had all week.

Chapter Five

Dawn had barely pierced the sky when Derica woke. Something heavy lay across her stomach and for a breath of time she didn't know what. Then she remembered the previous evening, and where she was. She smiled with languid pleasure, thinking about what she'd done. What *they'd* done, she and Kailen.

He slept soundly, lightly snoring beside her, his arm thrown over her in casual possession. She'd never been a woman who'd wanted to be possessed by a man. No woman got where she was without knowing how to grasp and maintain the upper hand in relationships, and frankly, no man had ever interested her enough to make her want to change her attitude. The men she worked with hadn't wanted a relationship with her except in the most primal sense—where they, of course, had the control. Not for her, thanks. The least she'd settle for was equality of power.

She could have had that with some of her previous lovers, she supposed. None of them had been involved with her firm directly, and so there'd been some freedom for her give in to the wantonness that lay below her controlled exterior. But she hadn't wanted to. Deep inside she'd felt the desire to let go though, and that's what Kailen tapped into. Tapped into, drilled into, drove into… As the metaphors came to mind, heat flared between her legs.

Taking a breath, she pulled herself toward the edge of the bed, sliding from under his arm. He made an effort to hold her, wrinkling his face and grunting as his fingers scrabbled for her body, but he didn't waken. When what he searched for wasn't there, he pulled his hand up under his chin and began snoring again.

Derica found the bathroom and relieved herself, then examined her reflection in the mirror over the sink. After their sessions of sex late in the afternoon, they'd fallen asleep only to waken hungry for each other hours later. That sequence repeated itself early in the morning, when she'd brought him to life with her mouth and ridden him to climax minutes later.

Neither food nor drink had entered her mind since arriving, and if they'd occurred to Kailen, he hadn't indicated it. Instead, only sex and sleep, then more sex, had occupied her consciousness. The alley cat analogy came to mind again, especially when she remembered the gleam in his eyes when she'd looked over her shoulder at him, her ass stuck in the air, an invitation to do whatever he wanted. Oh, she'd felt wild.

She wanted to be wild again.

Despite the interrupted sleep she looked refreshed, rested. Content, even. Like a woman well-used. She smiled at her reflection, knowing she had given as good as she got.

Tempted to go back to bed and wake him, she fought the urge. Her body cried for a different type of relief, and she decided to make coffee and see what Kailen had in the fridge.

Tiptoeing from the bathroom, she saw a shirt thrown across a chair near the bed. Like the one he'd worn the previous afternoon, this one was denim, but without the spatters of paint. She slipped it on and was immediately engulfed in his scent: musk, light sweat and a hint of oil paint. No other man in the world smelled like Kailen, and for a moment she was overpowered, feeling his hands on her body and the brush of his tongue on her clit. The intensity nearly robbed her of breath.

She buttoned the shirt and rolled up the sleeves, then left Kailen in bed to explore his home.

Coffee was easy to find, and she started a pot brewing. The loft was surprisingly warm, even so early and with the primarily northern exposure, and she was comfortable wandering around in her bare feet and half-dressed. In a pantry, she found a trash can and loaded it with the pizza boxes and empty cans that littered the table, then she rinsed the dishes left in the sink and stacked them in the dishwasher. Nodding approval, she noted the kitchen looked clean and neat.

With a steaming cup of coffee she walked through the rest of the loft. When she'd passed through the previous afternoon, clutter seemed to be everywhere. Upon more careful examination, she saw that clutter was all it was. The loft was as clean as her apartment. It was simply layered with…things. Clothes, books, empty cups—it was all there, in the living quarters. Only the studio was scrupulously neat, with everything in a particular niche.

The early morning light lent a touch of mystery to paintings stacked against one of the walls. Squatting, she looked at each, pulling a canvas forward to lean on her knee as she examined the one behind it.

She recognized Noelani and Fauve in a few. Others featured strangers. Several depicted a man and woman, or a man with two women. With a pain she shouldn't have felt, she admitted the man looked remarkably like Kailen. And he was depicted doing what he had done with her, last night and last week. Jealousy, hard and stinging, raged through her. Quickly, she shoved those paintings aside and flipped through another, smaller stack.

She remembered he'd said he worked for local designers, and these must be some of the contracted work. There were landscapes of the Bay area and still lifes.

"Do you like what you see?" His voice was hushed, or maybe it just seemed so, in the dim and quiet room. Yet, he'd startled her.

Standing, she wanted to gather her thoughts before facing him. He didn't give her the chance to turn, coming behind her and pulling her back against him with an arm around her waist. She leaned her head on his shoulder and cradled her cup with both hands in order not to spill. He had a cup in his left hand and sipped as he waited for her answer.

"I do like them. Even your landscapes have a sense of richness that's almost seductive." She smiled as she felt his cock rise against her back, knowing her words and her closeness inspired his reaction. "I don't know how you inspire sensuality with a painting of flowers or the Golden Gate Bridge, but you do."

"Hmm. You're the first person ever to express it that way. I like it." He set his cup on the work table then put hers beside it before turning her in his arms. "By the way, paintings aside, you look damn sexy in my shirt."

She took in the fact that he wore briefs and an open bathrobe and nothing else. His hair was tousled from sleep and his cheek, as it rubbed hers, was scratchy with the bristles of a beard. Tilting her head, she encouraged his exploration of her neck with his tongue and lips.

"I feel pretty sexy in it." She slid her hands under his robe and to his back.

He pulled her closer. "I almost hate to ask you to take it off, but I'm hungry."

Disappointment clouded her mind. She was getting all hot and bothered, and he was thinking *doughnuts*? "Oh, so you want me to get dressed."

Chuckling, he tilted her head back. "Not yet, sweetheart. Just take off the shirt. Let's satisfy one appetite at a time. First, into the shower. It's huge—lots of room to…eat. Then we can get dressed and go out for something more conventional."

"I do like the way you think." Snuggling against his body, she virtually purred. "Lead me to the shower! I feel a sudden urge to get all wet and soapy."

A quick movement of his hand made her gasp.

"You're already wet. Let's go work on the soapy part."

* * * *

Kailen posed and looked into the camera, but he wasn't concentrating on how to look good in the suit he modeled for the department store catalogue. Instead, his thoughts were on Derica and how many hours remained before he'd see her that night.

He couldn't believe how much his life had changed in the past two weeks. What had started as simple physical attraction had quickly turned into a red-hot passion that separation hadn't extinguished. Being apart that first week had only made him want her more, a fact that didn't particularly make him feel at ease. He liked being a free spirit, painting beautiful women in his own evocative style without having to worry how a wife or girlfriend would—or could—complicate things. More, having been a member of the rat race for years himself, he appreciated what it took to climb the corporate ladder. Being involved with a man who modeled, rode a courier bike around town for a living and painted nude women, wasn't the kind of man who would help Derica's career. He worried about that for her because he remembered so well what it took. He knew for certain he could never go back to that life, and so he could never ask her to compromise what she wanted in her life.

As difficult as it had been not to call after leaving her apartment that first night, he'd known instinctively it was for the best. When he'd answered the door the following Saturday, distracted at being interrupted, he couldn't believe she'd come to him. And stayed.

Now he fought the hard-on that sprang to life when he remembered the good, long time in the shower that Sunday morning. Her breasts weren't big or full, but they filled his hands and were a tender mouthful, too. Enjoying them had occupied several minutes before he'd soaped her, smoothing his hands over her slick body until she moaned with need.

When he lifted her over his erection and pressed her against the tile wall, neither of them had considered a condom. They'd thought only of hot water sluicing off bodies and steam filling the shower stall, as though it emanated from their fiery frenzy. Pounding hearts matched their bodies as they came together. Loving her without a rubber was just as he'd thought it would be—pure bliss as his cock drove into her over and over until she came with volcanic-like contractions, and tremors that shook them both.

Later, when breath had been caught and heart rates returned to normal, she'd assured him that she was on birth control and health issues were discussed to mutual satisfaction. More than satisfactorily for Kailen, since it meant that whenever they fucked he would feel her orgasm with no barriers. Now that he knew how it felt when her muscles clenched his cock, he didn't ever want to go back to being sheathed in latex. Skin to skin, her cream coating him and his cum filling her—that's the only way it should be between them. The mere thought made his rigid cock ache even more now. If he didn't do something to distract his body, he'd have to call for a break.

During breakfast that Sunday, when she'd reverted to her public, more conservative self, he'd explained again why he thought they shouldn't see each other any longer, although now that he'd had her—really had her—he'd been loath to tell her she should stay away. Her arrival at his loft had struck him in a way he hadn't been prepared for.

When he'd made his case to say goodbye, she'd looked at him with her big brown eyes that turned soft and warm rather than heated, and said, "I need you," and he'd felt a stab of joy that was completely unexpected.

They hadn't gone to her apartment since that first night. She seemed to prefer the careless mess of his place to the pronounced neatness of hers, and he didn't mind. Her apartment was her life without him, whereas his place represented somewhere she wanted to be, with him.

That Sunday he'd cancelled plans with friends so he and Derica could be together. She'd stripped then donned his shirt as soon as they'd gotten home. They'd read the newspaper together on the sofa, and when she stretched out for a nap, he'd sketched her.

Another quick drawing, this in one of his dress shirts, with the tie hanging loose and the top buttons undone, depicted Derica raising the hem of the shirt to show off the vee of brown curls at the juncture of her thighs, while her smile held no question as to what she demanded of the viewer. He loved the look of her, the feel of her, the sheer animalism she exhibited. And how she made him feel when he was with her, as well as inside her.

In the past two weeks, they'd been active lovers, though at her insistence she hadn't remained at his apartment overnight again. He assumed it was her effort to keep the two parts of her life separate, and at the beginning he hadn't minded, had even thought it best.

Between and around episodes of mind-blowing sex, they'd had long conversations and shared jokes. He started to look forward to her visits, and felt unreasonable pangs of disappointment on days when she called to say she wouldn't be coming over. Their ordinary talks about what had happened since they'd last been together took on a special importance, even when they meant delaying painting until later.

The closer they became, the more selfish Kailen felt about her. And possessive. Trouble was, he wanted her to feel selfish and possessive about him, too. When he put her in a cab after making love, it hurt to see her go. He wanted her to be in his life for more than a few hours a week, wanted to wake up with her every morning. God, he had it bad. How would he ever be able to let her go?

Under the glare of the camera lights, where everything was visible, Kailen hoped the secret he held didn't show in his face. That he'd started to fall in love.

* * * *

Finally, her knock sounded at the door. Kailen grinned when he opened it to find her flushed and nervous. Reaching out, he pulled her into the apartment.

"What's wrong?" He took her large shoulder bag from her and tossed it on the couch.

Her eyes followed its path and he knew if she'd been in her apartment, the purse would have had a place set aside just for it. He had a feeling being able to toss the bag wherever it was convenient was one of the things she liked about being in his home.

She looked back at him, trying out a smile. It didn't quite work, so he bent for a quick kiss.

Derica took a deep breath and looked calmer. "This is the first time we're going out with your friends."

He rubbed his thumb across her cheek and smiled. "You've met Noelani and Fauve. My friends are...friendly." There. He'd gotten her to smile.

"I know, but here, it's like a cocoon. I see them when you're working, not socially. What if-if they don't like me? I mean to talk to."

Insecure? His corporate maven? "Hey, two weeks ago you stepped in front of the cameras for a major advertising campaign and hardly blinked an eye. This is just drinks and dancing at a club with a few people I know. Nothing to be frightened about. I'll be with you." He hugged her to him.

"I know that logically." She stood quietly for a moment. "Where is it we're going again?" Her voice was stronger, with no hint of nervousness.

He pulled away and critically appraised what she wore. "The AG Club. That stands for 'Anything Goes,' in case you wondered, and for this club, you're a bit overdressed.

"Overdressed? But I—"

Within seconds he'd removed her bra, turned and tucked the waistband of the skirt to make it shorter and tugged it lower on her hips. He removed her panties, leaving them on the floor.

"There."

"Kailen, I can't possibly go out in public without panties or bra."

"Sure you can." He rubbed the back of his hand across her breast and smiled at the immediate reaction of her nipple to his touch. God, he loved how she always seemed to want him. He certainly couldn't get enough of her. "When we dance tonight I want to feel you with as little between us as possible. In those killer heels, your nipples will be right against mine." He leaned forward to kiss her.

Ignoring her look of trepidation, he led her out the door.

* * * *

The cab ride from Kailen's apartment had been a new experience. When Derica slid across the seat, her skirt had covered her ass, but just barely. Getting out was a different story. Kailen held out his hand, then watched her skirt slide up almost to her hips as she climbed from the back seat. Fortunately, he'd positioned himself so no one behind him could see a thing.

"You're so beautiful," he whispered in her ear, and a warm feeling flowed through her at his words.

The soft cotton of his shirt brushed her arm, and she thought that even in simple jeans and an old, worn shirt, he was more handsome than any man she'd ever seen. The diamond stud twinkled between strands of black hair covering his ear, and the rough, unshaven look she'd come to expect added to his sheer masculinity.

The erotic magnetism she'd felt for him from the beginning had evolved into a full-fledged addiction for her. While at work she found herself obsessing over him and when they could be together again. When she was with him, well, she didn't think. Their time together was magical, even beyond the sex, although that was more fantastic than anything she'd ever imagined.

Twice he'd voiced concerns that being seen with him wasn't good for her career. As straight-laced as MiBar was, she agreed with him. But except for the night of the party, they hadn't exactly been in a position to be "seen." Tonight was an exception, but she doubted anyone in her company would be caught dead in a place like the AG Club.

After their first breakfast out, she'd either cooked or brought food in when she went to his apartment. For the rest of the time, they'd subsisted on each other with a burning passion that hadn't shown any indication of abating. Her breath quickened with the thought of how many times they'd made love, the different positions they'd employed and the way he never failed to bring her to crashing orgasms.

Lately though, sharing a quiet conversation while they fixed a meal brought her satisfaction as great as what she felt in bed. She told him of her day, and the interest shining in his eyes warmed her. He told her of something funny that happened on his courier route and the laughter they enjoyed was as good as a kiss. The closeness between them was a warm caress, like when he wrapped her in his arms after making love. She'd never felt like this before.

"Are you all right?" Kailen looked at her with amusement in his eyes.

She smiled. "Just thinking."

"About something good, obviously."

"Oh, yes!"

He guided her to the front of the club, but still managed to lean to her ear. "About me?"

"Ha! You're not the center of the universe." *Just the center of my universe.*

The thought stunned her. Sometime in the last two weeks, Kailen had crossed the line between a fling out of her normally controlled, organized world into something she didn't think she could live without. She didn't want to try to, anyway.

As though reading her mind he whispered, "I don't need to be the center of all universes, just yours." He paid the cover charge and started toward the door.

She stopped him and reached up to touch his face, not smiling now. He looked into her eyes. The world stopped turning for that moment.

"I wasn't looking for a center. But nothing has been the same since that night at the hotel."

He didn't say anything. Derica was aware of people moving around them, but Kailen didn't seem to mind or care. It was as close as she'd ever come to telling a man she loved him, and she couldn't tell from his expression if he was happy or sad, or if he even understood what she had tried to say.

Then she could tell. He looked miserable. Oh, God. What had she done? Obviously, he didn't feel the same about her, and now nothing *would* be the same.

She forced a smile. "Come on. Your friends will be wondering about us." Tugging his hand, she pulled him into the club.

Once their eyes adjusted to the dimly lit interior, Kailen nodded to a man who waved to them from a table across the room. With her hand in his, he led her through the maze of packed tables.

In contrast to the seating area, the dance floor was bright with strobe lights cutting the darkness, highlighting everything but lighting nothing. By the time her mind registered what she saw on the floor, the light had moved on, leaving her unsure.

The music was canned and loud, and Kailen had to talk into her ear in order for her to catch the names of his friends. Michael, Danny, and

Nick smiled and nodded as Kailen pointed to them. Noelani and Fauve smiled and wiggled their fingers.

The woman on her right, Sandra, gave her a critical look with no hint of friendliness. For a moment, Derica was caught by Sandra's striking looks. Black eyes set in olive skin matched the color of her hair, which hung like loose, shimmering satin down her back. Unlike Noelani, she wasn't petite. Instead, her body was voluptuous and curvy. Something vaguely familiar concerning the unfriendly woman pushed at the back of Derica's mind, but she couldn't grasp it. Like Kailen's paintings, the woman's bearing emitted sex even while she sat there, unmoving.

"Nick is my brother," Kailen said, and she took a longer look at the man sitting on the other side of Sandra.

There was a resemblance in the dark hair and build. But his eyes were brown, not blue, and his face was softer, fuller, without the strength of Kailen's features.

Nick turned toward Sandra, pointing at her empty glass. She nodded and he got up, looking at Kailen with a raised brow.

"Drink?" Kailen mouthed to Derica.

"Wine, please," she shouted.

He squeezed her shoulder as he left the table and moved toward the bar with Nick.

"Derica, you're going to love the AG Club," Fauve yelled from her spot on the other side of Michael. Her hair was held off her face with sequined barrettes that matched the sparkly buttons on her gauzy blouse.

The buttons weren't the only distraction on the blouse. Behind the single layer of material, her ample breasts could be seen quite clearly.

The music changed to a faster tempo, and Fauve shouted, "Whoo!" and threw her arms over her head, clapping to the beat. With a grin at Michael, she stood and moved to the dance floor. Laughing, he got up to follow.

Danny said something into Noelani's ear. She looked at Derica, then shot a glance at Sandra. Flattening her lips in a worried expression, she said something back. Danny shook his head before answering, and with a flash of an apologetic smile at Derica, she stood to let him lead her to the floor. Noelani's blouse at least was opaque, but Derica saw with dismay that her skirt was little more than a wide belt. Even without underwear, she felt more clothed than Fauve and Noelani.

Alone at the table with Sandra, Derica turned to her. Raising her voice she said, "This is an interesting place." It was an inane comment, but considering how difficult it was to talk over the music, she felt it was the best she could do.

Sandra shrugged then tapped her manicured nails on the table and stared at the dancers. The cut of her gold satin blouse showed the curve of her breasts. Her curled lip and attitude of total disdain added to her allure, and for the first time, Derica understood the term "sex pot."

"Have you been friends with Nick and Kailen for long?"

Sandra turned her black gaze on Derica and smiled, but without humor. "Years. I was one of Kailen's first models." She waited.

Was she waiting to find out how Derica would respond? Derica didn't know what to say, but she could now place the woman. In the paintings she'd thought Kailen was part of, the ones that had made her jealous, this woman was featured. Try as she might, she knew she could never like Sandra, and it had nothing to do with the way she was acting there at the club.

Sandra studied her. "You know what kind of paintings he creates, don't you?"

"Yes, of course I do." Derica raised her head and faced the woman's insolent stare squarely.

"Well then, you know how intimately he knows his models. He's a wonderful artist, but he's *very* good at making sure his models get everything they need. Or want." With a sneer, she turned away again.

Derica blazed with sudden anger. How dare this woman talk about her Kailen like that, as though he belonged to her. He didn't. And he never would if Derica could only convince him to love her.

Before she could formulate a reply that suited her mood, the men returned. Kailen slid into the chair beside her after depositing their drinks on the table. He put his arm across her shoulders and pulled her close. She took a deep breath. He wore no cologne, but the light scent of soap and the ever-present hint of paint filled her nostrils. This was Kailen. Her Kailen.

Her man.

Immediately she calmed. Sliding closer to him, she shot a glance to her side and took some pleasure in the stare of enmity Sandra aimed at her. *Take that, you bitch.*

"What do you think?" His voice was pitched to be heard by her alone.

"Loud." In fact, the bass seemed to vibrate through her in a not unpleasant way. Like jungle drums, the rich beat inspired an answering throb deep in her belly. That throb called for Kailen.

She took a gulp of wine, knowing the combination of alcohol, hot rhythm and Kailen could be explosive, but wanting to take the chance. His earlier response showed he didn't love her, but she could make him want her. That much she'd proven in the past two weeks. She'd take what she could get.

"Let's dance, Kailen." The voice came from her right.

Startled at the intrusion, she turned to find Sandra standing with an outstretched hand to Kailen. Nick stared into his drink, his mouth pulled into a thin line. Kailen's arm tightened around her shoulders.

"No thanks, Sandra." Holding up his drink he said, "Cheers." He clinked his glass against Derica's glass and met his brother's eyes as they tapped glasses. Sandra sat, but stared toward the dance floor.

Kailen took a sip then stood, pulling Derica from her seat. "Come on, let's see what you can do out there, Lady Executive."

She strolled to the edge of the floor ahead of him, making sure her hips swayed with each step. Lights swooped across the floor, making the unlit spots seem even darker than they were. It took a moment to focus and she turned to him for guidance. With a surety of step, he led her to a bare spot.

A swath of light sliced across his face and the hunger in his eyes cut through her. Raising her arms over her head, she let the fast beat of the music take control. With a life of their own, her hips gyrated in time to the rhythm. The sudden darkness provided a pocket of privacy even on the crowded floor, and she felt his hands on her hips, pulling her closer, matching her twists and rolls with his own hips. His erection rubbed against her, enticing her, tempting her, even through her clothes.

She dropped her arms linking her fingers behind his head. Deliciously, painfully slowly his hands inched from her hips to her breasts where his thumbs coaxed her nipples to aching, rigid peaks.

They weren't alone in their exploration. A short distance away, Michael suckled Fauve's bare breast, and on the other side a man and his partner appeared to be screwing as they danced. She turned her head back and Kailen took her lips in a deep, searching kiss. Her blood raced. She wanted him like she'd never wanted anything in her life. She groaned into his mouth, knowing he couldn't hear it over the music, but hoping he could feel it.

Suddenly, the music stopped. All lights on the dance floor went out. Seconds later, a slow number began. Without the moving strobes criss-crossing the room, it was surprising how lighting from the table area illuminated the dance floor. When he raised his head, Derica saw Kailen's hooded eyes had darkened. He wrapped his hands over her butt and pulled her closer, until she almost forgot where they were.

Like a well-choreographed dance, they swayed together, her hips grinding his, her nipples scraping his chest.

"God, I want you," he said into her ear. Reaching under her skirt, he stroked her cheeks. She spread her legs enough for him to slip his fingers between her lips. "You're so wet." Leaning back so he could look at her, he asked, "Have you ever made love in a public place?"

Shocked yet titillated, she shook her head. Licking her lips, she glanced at the slowly moving couples around them.

"Come on." He took her hand and pulled her off the floor. Behind their table, a hallway extended to the back of the building. A few feet along the hall was a short offshoot.

A black pay phone hung on one side. Kailen backed her up opposite it. His tongue filled her mouth while his fingers fumbled with the buttons on her blouse, then his shirt. Skin to skin, he pushed against her, side to side and up until she stretched on her toes to meet him. She felt his hands fumbling with the button, then lowering the zipper on his jeans. His firm hands grasped her thighs and pushed her skirt to her hips. With his hand under her knee, he brought her leg to his waist, then thrust into her in one swift drive.

"Oh!" From a distance she heard people passing, even making comments about the couple fucking by the pay phone, but nothing mattered except this need, this itch, the feeling of completeness she felt when Kailen filled her. Each hard thrust took her a step closer to climax.

"I think Sandra would like to be where I am now," she said in his ear, panting to get the words out. The way the woman had looked at Kailen, as though she owned him, tore at Derica. If that was him with her in the painting….

He grunted. "She's a bitch. Nick should drop her."

"She wants you." The thought of people around them, their public display, the reassurance that Kailen was here with her, pushed her on. Just a little more and she'd be free of this burning ache low in her belly.

"She's a bitch in heat. She wants every man. Except Nick, and that's what drives him crazy. It's been that way since they met, modeling for me." He raised his head, holding himself still inside her. "Do you wish it was her with me instead of you?"

Her low, hard laugh took her by surprise. "I'd pull out every strand of her hair if I found her back here with you. And then I'd get nasty."

His chuckle warmed her. "That's my girl." Then his smile disappeared. His gaze dropped to her lips and he took them in an almost savage conquest. His cock drove into her, giving her everything she craved.

The metal of his zipper teased the tender skin of her thighs. His open mouth found her shoulder where he sucked and then scraped her with his teeth. Without warning she felt herself soaring. She held her breath, trembling, unable to speak or even moan. But Kailen moaned, pressing his forehead to hers, pulsing inside her and holding himself rigid as he climaxed.

He dropped her leg and sagged against her. "I don't think I can move."

Breathing in short, shallow pants, coming down from her own high, she knew how he felt. With effort, she raised her arms to wrap around his back. Someone behind them cleared his throat. Kailen pushed away from the wall and turned, shielding her with his body.

"Thanks for the show," a soft voice said, then footsteps moved off.

He heaved a sigh and smiled at her. Zipping his pants as she did up her blouse he asked, "Did you know he was there?"

"Not really, although I know people saw us." She grinned. "I should be scandalized, but it was damned exciting."

Buttoning his shirt, he gave her a serious look. "Suppose this had been someplace where your colleagues hung out. Would it still have been exciting?"

Her breath caught at the thought. "Well, the situation would be different. I wouldn't go anywhere dressed like this where company people would be, it-it just wouldn't have happened, is all."

He nodded as though he'd expected that answer.

She touched his arm. "It was really something, but...you understand, don't you?"

With a gentle kiss on her cheek, and his fingers furrowing her hair, he whispered, "I understand completely."

Chapter Six

The last week had been different from the previous two. Knowing he loved Derica made each moment with her precious, every moment apart like something was missing inside him. He'd never felt that way before, even when he'd met and married Emily, years ago when he'd been very young and dumb as shit. Steven, as everyone thought of him back then, had *thought* he was in love, but he hadn't even known the meaning of the word. Neither had Emily.

Just out of grad school, they believed they had the world all figured out. Mutual friends had introduced them, and they'd immediately become lovers. Marriage a couple of months later seemed just the thing, and he'd ignored warnings from family that they didn't know each other well enough.

Taking a job at a big advertising firm was a way to use his art and make decent money while he gained a reputation as a painter. Emily dabbled in real estate, an acceptable part-time position that allowed her to make a splash in society, as her wealthy parents expected her to do.

After two years, when Steven decided his dream of art had to take precedence over a career in business, neither Emily nor her parents were happy. Once his decision had been made, the marriage hadn't lasted another six months. A short time later, Emily had become a corporate vice president's wife and he'd become Kailen.

The experience had given him a healthy respect for what the business world demanded of someone with ambition, and what was accepted in that arena. It had also taught him what love wasn't, which is how he now recognized what it was.

No matter how much Derica denied it, his lifestyle, his work, his friends—none of it fit what she needed to push ahead and succeed. Deep inside, she knew it, too. That had been painfully obvious in her response to his question last week at the club. His forays into exhibitionism were certainly limited, but the AG Club and places like it were part of his social life. They most definitely were not part of hers. He didn't see how she could keep a foot in both worlds and find real happiness in either. Eventually she would make a choice, and why wouldn't she choose what she'd worked years to attain?

Sighing as he finished dressing, he reminded himself that he'd never actually told Derica he loved her. Of course, she hadn't told him, either, which in his mind confirmed that she was really only comfortable with what they had physically—and only then if it was removed from her job and colleagues. They never even went to her apartment, for Christ's sake, a place that reflected her true nature. No, when it came down to holding her back from what she'd worked her whole life to achieve, or letting her go, he'd let her go. Real love didn't keep someone from their dreams. That was an Emily Lesson.

Sticking his wallet in his back pocket, he picked up his keys from the dresser and took a long appraisal of himself in the mirror. Unusual for the weekends, he'd made a concession and shaved that morning, though he knew by afternoon he'd have the shadowed, dark look that characterized his commercial photos. He'd had his hair trimmed the previous afternoon so that it only grazed his ear lobes, one of which sported his trademark diamond stud. A black tee shirt and jeans, clean but worn.

He looked just a little rough, a bit non-traditional. Well, actually, the typical "bad boy" it was rumored good girls always fell for stared back at him. Since Derica was the only "good girl" he wanted and this was their first time with her colleagues since the night of the photo shoot, Kailen was uncharacteristically nervous. He looked the way she liked him to look—when they were on their own. But did he look right for her boss' home across the Bay? He shrugged at his reflection. It was a *picnic*, after all.

Scooping up a small package from the coffee table as he passed, he left the loft and headed for the garage across the street where he kept the car. As infrequently as he used the small vehicle, he wondered why he kept it at all. He found a good spot for the present—a painting—on the floor behind his seat. Pulling out into traffic, he wondered again if Derica would like it. In the time since they'd met, he hadn't given her a single gift, but he wanted her to have this.

She waited on the curb, saving him the effort of finding a parking space. Conservatively dressed in full-flowing, taupe-colored slacks and a short-sleeved, coral-colored cotton sweater, with patent leather flats, Kailen noted with resignation that she looked exactly like the professional woman she was, so unlike the woman of the previous week who had made love in the public hallway of a club, then taunted him the rest of the night with her cock-teasing dances and temping glances. There'd been nothing conservative about *that* woman.

It wasn't until she was ready to get in that Kailen noticed a large box on the sidewalk beside her. She put it in the back seat then climbed in the front.

"Hi." He smiled and leaned over to kiss her.

"Hi, back" she replied when he raised his head.

A horn blew behind them, and Kailen put his mind to driving.

"What's in the box?"

"The dress I wore at the photo shoot. It's not mine, I just rented it and I thought if you don't mind a detour I'd return it. It's a little out of the way though, in the three hundred block of Post."

"That's no problem." He made a right at the next corner, heading toward downtown instead of the bridge. "So, are you ready to face your friends again, dragging along the underwear model?"

"Lord! I'd forgotten all about that billboard, although I did pay more attention the week after the party. The funny thing is, once I started looking for it, I saw it everywhere."

He grinned at her. "And?"

"The real thing is *sooo* much better!"

Laughing out loud, he winked at her.

"No, seriously." She ran her hand up his thigh.

His muscles tightened at her touch, but he maintained his smile.

"All of the bicycling really pays off, and it shows in the ad, believe me."

Distracted by her fingers skimming to the top of his leg, he almost didn't stop for the red light at the bottom of the hill. His smile became strained.

Her fingers curved around his cock, which was now hard with need and aching to escape one enclosed space in order to invade another.

"But where your...attributes look so damn good blown up and plastered on those billboards"—she dropped her voice to a seductive low—"they *feel* like heaven."

"I swear to God, Derica," he ground out through clenched teeth, "I'm going to pull into the darkest corner of the darkest parking garage and have my dirty way with you if you don't stop right now." The light changed and once again Kailen was prodded into action only when horns blew behind him.

"Promises, promises," she said with a laugh, but she removed her hand. "You need to do a better job keeping your mind on driving."

"Yeah, thanks," he muttered.

"You haven't commented on how I look," she said with a pout in her voice.

"You look beautiful and you know it. The business woman out for an afternoon tea."

She slapped his arm playfully. "Even when a woman knows she looks all right, it's nice to hear her man say it."

Her man. Definitely what he wanted but was afraid to count on.

"This is different from what I usually wear. We'll see if The Wives approve. Their nod is even more important now, with the promotion being decided."

His attention jumped into high gear. "Promotion? You haven't said anything about a promotion."

Frowning, she looked at the street sign as they zipped through an intersection. "I haven't? It's big—something I've really hoped for. Daniel told me about it the week after that client party we went to. They've been deciding for weeks now and I heard it's come down to me and Joel Miller." She pointed out the windshield. "There's the shop, up in the next block on the right."

"Will you be long?"

"No, I don't think so. Believe me, it's not the kind of place that'll have crowds."

"I'll circle the block, then." He turned on the four-way flashers and double parked while she got the box out of the backseat. Fortunately, she must not have seen his package because she hadn't pressed him about it. Later, after he took her home, there would be time enough to give it to her and talk.

And they'd talk in *her* apartment, where she could feel the dichotomy of their positions. As much as he didn't want to lose her, each day he needed her more. The longer they went on, the harder the break would be when it happened. He felt torn, not wanting to give her up, but not enjoying knowing the loss was coming regardless of what he wanted. It would almost be better to force the point.

When he approached the area for the second time, he saw her come out of a small dress shop. His heart raced and he felt an idiotic smile fight its way to the surface, just like it did every time he saw her.

She tossed a wrapped box of some sort on the floor of the backseat before getting in.

"I forgot to tell you. It's Hannah McNaught's birthday. That's the reason for the backyard barbeque. I was lucky. They had a wonderful scarf that I picked up for a song."

Kailen remembered Hannah was Derica's boss' wife, and that she'd given Derica a hard time when he'd accompanied her to the company party. Given that, he already had a bad impression of the woman, but he would have brought her a gift—a little still life or something—if he'd known it was her birthday. In fact, he could send her some token next week. A surprise like that might go some distance toward helping Derica get that promotion.

"I thought we were going to a casual picnic, not a special event. Am I dressed all right?" He felt her eyes on him.

"You're going to stand out like a sore thumb."

Shit! The last thing he wanted was to embarrass her. He frowned, wondering if they had time to cut back to his apartment so he could change.

"The women are going to fight like hellions to get near you, and the men will hope whatever you've got will rub off a little on them." She smoothed her hands across his shoulders. "I think you look perfect."

The tension he'd felt all morning flowed from him. "Well then, if you're happy, I'm happy."

"Trust me," she said as she leaned toward him, "I'm happy." With a flick of her tongue and gentle press of her lips, she kissed his cheek.

The idiotic smile made its way to the surface again. He only wished they could stay happy.

With a glance in the rearview mirror, he saw the store Derica had just come out of shimmer in the morning sun and vanish. He slammed on the brakes and turned to focus his attention on the spot where the store had been. The squeal caused by the car behind him as it skidded to a halt went unheard, as did the horn blaring when the irate driver pulled around him. Where the store had been, he was *certain*, two other shops now abutted: Johnson's Jewels and Sweet Secrets. He shook his head, ignoring Derica's puzzled frown. He suddenly had a bad feeling about the day. A premonition that, like the dress shop, his hopes would soon disappear.

Then the memory of the shop faded from his mind.

* * * *

The afternoon had warmed nicely. But then, it was always warmer on this side of the Bay. Derica rocked lazily in a wicker chair on the back patio. Sausalito was a great place to live, and this house was the best of the best. Set on a hillside, the front boasted unmatched views of San Francisco and the Bay, and the back climbed up the hillside in terraced levels. Her eyes half closed, she thought she could live here, unmoving, the rest of her life if someone would bring her food and drink at regular intervals. And Kailen. She wouldn't want to live here or anywhere without Kailen.

She watched him as he played badminton with the handful of children who'd come to Hannah's birthday cook-out. Just as she'd predicted, none of the men had come in tee shirts, choosing instead polos, or even dress shirts with their Dockers and slacks. The couple of braver souls who'd shown up in jeans wore designer labels. Derica was sure they'd never consider sitting on the grass in them, not for something as trivial as showing the McNaught's granddaughter a butterfly as it made its rounds along the row of daisies and dahlias. Not like Kailen had.

As soon as they'd entered the house, she could almost smell the arousal from some of the women. If Victoria Haber had literally licked her lips in anticipation of eating him, it wouldn't have surprised Derica. Instead, Victoria satisfied herself by latching onto Kailen immediately, taking charge of introducing him to the mixed group of family and company employees. The men had eyed him warily, as though they, too, scented the change in the room and were uncertain of how to handle it.

Kailen dealt with their visit in the most perfect manner, charming the women and making "man talk" with the guys, remarkably antagonizing no one. Before dinner the men had found their way into the den to watch the obligatory game. It surprised her that even Joel Miller, the man with whom she was in competition for the promotion, followed the group into the den. How many times had he told her he hated football? Yet there he went, like a sheep.

Instead of joining the men in the den, Kailen played catch in the backyard with the six or seven children who'd come with their parents. At the few other casual social events she'd attended, she didn't remember anyone paying attention to the children, and they were thrilled with the notice.

As she watched, Kailen played with the children, and Victoria and a couple of other women hanging on the sidelines played with the thought of Kailen playing with them. *Fat chance.* Flashing her smiles when he caught her eye and taking her aside for a scorching kiss when he came in to wash up for dinner, he left little doubt who was on his mind.

He'd relaxed with her after their meal, until the older boys—eight or nine years old, she guessed—cajoled him into a match of badminton. Then, with a smile as his apology, he'd gone off to swat the birdie over the net until now, when the kids looked ready to collapse.

"Time for cake!" Martha, Hannah and Daniel's daughter, called to the group.

Derica stretched her arms over her head and forced herself out of her indulgent, lazy mood. When she stood, she glimpsed Martha disappearing into the dining room where the two of them had earlier arranged the cake and gifts. The elaborately decorated cake with its discreet single candle was visible from the patio, while the table piled high with wrapped presents stood to the side. She hoped Martha's son had retrieved her gift from the car and placed it with the rest of the packages, but as she directed her gaze to the tall, dark-haired man making his way from the lower lawn, she could think of only one gift *she* wanted unwrapped. A quick glance at her watch showed they couldn't leave quite yet. But soon…

Whoops of glee greeted the announcement of birthday cake, and the children dropped their rackets as one and headed for the house at a run. Kailen followed at a more sedate pace, but looked no less eager.

"You like cake, huh?" she said when he met her on the patio and gave her a hug.

"If it's chocolate," he said with a note of hopefulness.

She shook her head, and his smile drooped.

"It's okay. I'm just happy to find a way to end the game. Usually I can handle opponents under ten with no trouble, but this bunch was about to wear me out."

Laughing, she pulled the door open. "Yes, it looked like it."

He dragged her into the small washroom just inside and kicked the door shut with his heel. Wrapping his arms around her, he looked into her eyes. "Actually, I'm better at other games."

"I know that very well." Evidence of the kind of game he was great at poked her in the stomach. She rubbed against him.

"Watch it, woman! Today is the longest time we've been with each other and yet not, if you know what I mean. We've hardly even kissed, so you can imagine the state I'm in. Don't tempt me unless you want to handle the consequences."

"I want to handle every consequence you've got."

He groaned and crushed her to him then used his tongue to explore her lips and mouth. Her pulse raced and her blood caught fire flowing through her body. She felt her nipples harden, even as her breasts flattened against his chest.

A knock at the door stopped what would have logically followed. Only with effort could she suck enough air to say, "Just a minute," in a half-way normal tone.

Martha's voice floated through the door. "That's all right, Derica. I wondered where you were, is all. Mother's opening her gifts and I could use your help serving the cake around all the activity."

"Yes, I understand." She hadn't taken her arms from his neck. His hold heated her. God! Their clothes would combust if she didn't step away soon. His breath on her forehead was fast and shallow—he was as affected as she—and that knowledge only made her desire greater.

"I'll-I'll be right there, Martha." There was no longer anything normal about her tone. Only someone who had never had sex wouldn't recognize the huskiness and strain. Martha had a child, ergo…

There was silence on the other side of the door, then she heard, "Hmph!" and footsteps dying away as she left.

Kailen grunted. "Like mother like daughter, I see." He bent his head to lick the tender skin on her neck.

"I've got to go," she whispered, still not breaking away.

"Mm-hmm."

Taking a deep breath, she pushed away from him. "What am I going to do with you?"

He raked his hands through his hair and sighed. "Well, I had an idea."

She smiled. "Later."

He cocked his head. "I guess it will have to be." Giving her a quick kiss he added, "You go ahead. I'm not in any shape to be seen in public yet."

She nodded and slipped out. Calming her breath and straightening her clothes, she wondered yet again how she would find the courage to come right out and say she loved him. She wondered in fact if she could. Until today, she'd managed to keep their worlds separate, and she liked it like that. But if they carved any future for themselves—even as lovers, like they were now—their worlds would have to collide sooner or later. That was her purpose in inviting him today. It was an opening gambit, to test the waters on both sides.

The day hadn't been a rousing success in that Kailen had remained apart from the men, but it hadn't been a disaster, either. He could simply be a quirky addition to the occasional corporate functions she was expected to attend. What they did outside her work environment was their secret, and had to stay that way. If The Wives, who had heart palpitations over a sexy party gown, ever got wind of how she dressed when she went out with Kailen, it would not be good for her. If they ever discovered what she did with him, it wouldn't be tolerated; people at MiBar had been dismissed for less than screwing in a public hallway. She'd been playing with fire and knew it. She just had to make sure she didn't get burned.

Time to think about that later.

She strolled into the party room and saw that several gifts were being passed around so that everyone could look them before they were set aside. Derica had never known an older woman who fussed so much over birthdays. From the look on Daniel's face, she thought he must feel the same way. He smiled wryly at her and raised a whiskey tumbler in a silent toast.

As she made her way around the edge of the table, a scream pierced the air. Panicked, she pushed through the crowd to Hannah, who stared at her in disgust, her mouth open, hand to her heart.

"What's wrong? Are you all right?" Derica took her arm and tried to get her to sit, but Hannah yanked her arm away.

"You-you…! How dare you give this to me!"

"What *is* it?" She looked at the table and saw what everyone else stared at. A small oil painting of her. Brown wrapping paper still clung to the bottom of the frame.

Unlike Kailen's usual style, the form wasn't blurred, so there really was no question regarding the identity of the model. She wasn't naked, but she might as well have been, since she wore nothing but Kailen's dress shirt. Only the last three buttons were secured and one smooth, alabaster breast with its dusky nipple stood exposed to the viewer. A necktie slashed with primary colors hung untied, streaks of vibrancy against the white of the shirt. Her head was twisted to the left and one hand raked through her hair while the other caressed her mound, the hem of the shirt pulled up enough to reveal the darkened triangle of curls.

The room turned deadly silent. For one moment, she couldn't remember to breathe. Her mind didn't grasp the trouble she was in, that the two worlds she'd held so carefully apart had now crashed into one another at the worst time. All she could think about was how well composed the artwork was, and how her lover had captured the sexiest essence of her.

Kailen!

Derica looked for him and saw his grim face watching her. "I'm sorry," he mouthed.

She shook her head.

"I want them out of my house!" Hannah broke the silence and suddenly everyone began talking.

Some adults ushered children from the room. Others, a good many of them men, pushed forward to get a better look at the oil. Daniel appeared beside her and reached for the painting, but Hannah snatched it from his reach. When she raised it above her head to smash it against the table, Derica found her strength and her voice.

"Don't, Hannah. That's mine." Reaching up, she firmly took the framed piece from the older women. "There's been a mistake."

"You're right, there has been." Hannah glared at her husband. "For years I've told you what kind of woman I thought she was, and now you see that I was right. And you were going to give her that promo—"

"Stop it, Hannah." His tone, modulated but firm, halted her mid-sentence. With a hand on her shoulder, he pushed her back into her seat. "Finish the party or not. I have business to take care of."

"Business with *her*, I imagine, now that you've seen what she's willing to do."

Uncomfortable, people began leaving the room. "Look what you've done," she said to Derica. "Look!"

Clutching her painting, Derica allowed Daniel to guide her to his study. She couldn't look at Kailen, couldn't imagine what this would do to her future and to them.

In seconds, she and Daniel were joined by three of the partners. They all looked dour. With a cry, she sank into a chair, envisioning all she'd worked for swirl down the drain like dirty bathwater.

Chapter Seven

For over an hour Kailen had alternately sat on Derica's apartment steps and paced the sidewalk in front. All he thought about was the expression on her face when she'd looked up at him. Horror, shame, resignation that she wouldn't get the promotion. Maybe acknowledgement that she might not keep her job. And it was all his fault.

Why the hell didn't I leave that damn thing at home and give it to her later? He knew why. He'd wanted her to see it in contrast to her apartment, her ordered life that reflected her ordered career. He wanted to shock her, to force her to see how different their lives were. Only after she recognized the stark contrast could she consider whether or not merging their lives was possible. It was too easy for them to let the difficult decisions slide in the comfort of his place. If she decided she couldn't be with him anymore, he didn't know how he would stand it, but better now than a month from now, when the pain would be that much worse. Only by startling her could he be sure she really understood the change she'd have to make.

Well, he'd startled her all right.

A cab pulled up and Derica got out, then leaned back in to pay the driver. When she turned and saw him, she nodded but didn't smile. She held the painting tightly to her chest, as she had when she left the room at the MacNaught's.

"Why didn't you stay?" She looked wrung out.

"I was ordered out by Hannah McNaught. She actually threatened to call the police if I waited out front for you, and"—he raked his hand through his thick, black hair—"frankly I was so pissed I started driving and when I looked up, I was here." He tried to gauge her attitude. It was strange, but she didn't seem too upset or angry. "I'm sorry I left you."

She shrugged. "It's okay. Come upstairs and talk."

Heaving a sigh of relief, he followed her inside. She didn't speak or try to touch him in the elevator, or after she'd opened the apartment door and locked it after him.

Tossing her purse on the coffee table, she sank onto the sofa and kicked off her shoes. He stood, uneasy at how unemotional she seemed. He'd never really seen her mad—was this the calm before the storm?

"Derica, I swear to God I didn't mean to embarrass you. Somehow—I don't know how—the wrapping on the two packages was so close they were almost identical. You picked up the wrong one."

She shook her head. "No, I asked Martha's son to bring in the package on the floor in the back of the car. I didn't know there were two."

"Shit! I'm sorry. I'm so damned sorry." He began to pace. His mind raced with what he could do to make everything better for her, but the only thing he could think of was… He gulped, took a deep breath and turned to her.

"Look, I don't have to model. If I didn't, I'd cut my hair. And I wasn't always a courier, you know. I actually had a real job, in an office." He smiled at her sudden look of interest. Kneeling beside the sofa, he took her hand in his. "I was actually quite good at commercial art, so money wouldn't be a problem for us. And painting can take a backseat in my life for a change."

Her eyes widened in shock. "What are you saying? You can't give up painting. It's what you *are*, not what you do." She glanced at the work she held. "But what you do is wonderful."

He was puzzled. "So, you'd be comfortable working at MiBar and being with me?"

"Oh, no." She laughed at what must have been utter confusion on his face. "I can't stay at MiBar, they fired me."

"*Fired* you?" Kailen surged to his feet and began pacing again.

"After telling me they'd decided to give me the promotion." Her voice sounded wistful.

"Bastards!"

To his surprise, she seemed to blow it all off. Crossing her ankles on the coffee table, she leaned back into the sofa. "Turns out, there's a morals clause in my employment contract. Who reads all the fine print, anyway?" She actually laughed.

He stopped pacing to stare at her in amazement.

"It's all right, Steven. We'll work things out, now that we know we love each other."

Steven? We love each *other*? Without a word he sat beside her, waiting for her to explain.

"I felt pretty awful when Daniel took me into the study. Mike Hawkins—remember him? The president of the company?"

Kailen nodded.

"He started, saying he understood what I did outside the office was my own business but that the painting showed him that I was engaged in activities that might end up in public, and which didn't fit the image the company wanted to portray. The fact that I'd brought the painting into the house where there were children…. Well, you can guess the rest. Daniel did everything he could for me, but with no luck."

She sighed, looking so sad he wanted to crush her to him, to comfort her.

"I was so disappointed, I can't even express it. I deserved that promotion, damn it! And for them to take it away over something that was none of their business?" She shook her head and took a breath before continuing. "Through most of it I sat listening, stunned that all I'd worked so hard for was disappearing, and then I looked at this." She held up the painting. "And I saw it."

"Saw what?" Hell, he wished she'd get to the point. He didn't think he could wait much longer to hear her say again that she loved him.

"The art. The intent behind what you'd painted. And this." Tapping her nail against the lower right-hand corner, she pointed to his name. "*S. Hooper*. Not Kailen, like you sign all of your work. There was more than sexuality in this work, there was something deeper. My features are sharp and clear. That shows how you think of me. This work is from Steven's heart, not Kailen's brush."

He grinned. "Yeah, but does it make you hot?"

Laughing, she grinned back. "You know it does." She put the painting in her lap. "Today hasn't been all bad news. They kind of know they're on thin ice because to my knowledge, that morals clause has never been used," she said. "No one can prove I posed for the painting or that I even knew it existed." She stared at him pointedly. "Which I didn't. So they gave me the severance package designated in my contract and a very nice...bonus, I guess you could call it," she said, grinning.

"I've heard of a hiring bonus, but never a firing bonus. Anyway, this is bribery, no doubt, but it'll get me over the hump until another job opens. I made a call to a friend on the way home and I don't think I'll be out of work for long."

Steven took the artwork and laid it on the table before pulling her onto his lap. "Say it, Derica, and I'll say it back."

She ran her fingers through his hair and gazed into his eyes. "I love you, Steven. I love you, Kailen. I love you, no matter what you call yourself."

Gently, his lips caressed hers. "I love you, Derica." He smiled against her lips. "But no one calls me Steven any more."

"I will," she vowed, "in moments of greatest passion." She wrapped her arms around his neck. "I think I feel such a moment coming on very soon."

"Do you?" He arranged her more comfortably over his cock.

"Make me call you Steven."

"I will, sweetheart. Right now."

* * * *

Derica couldn't sleep. It wasn't that she wasn't exhausted; she was, after the events of the day. But she was happy, too, and excited. The luminescent dial on the clock showed two in the morning. Steven snored softly beside her, but she knew if she got up he would wake, so she contented herself with lying there, absorbing his warmth.

Funny how easy it was thinking of him as Steven after the weeks of calling him Kailen. She loved that it was their name, their secret to share. Even his brother, Nick, referred to him as Kailen. But for her there would forever be a difference in her mind between Kailen and Steven, although they were the same wonderful man. *Her* man.

After making love on the sofa, they'd dressed and gone out for dinner. Over the meal he'd told her about his wife and how she'd tried to make him into something he wasn't. Her heart swelled that he'd been willing to make those changes for her when he thought it would help her. Derica had assured him that she could never ask him to give up his work. They'd find a way to work out their different lifestyles, no matter what it took, and maintain the essence of what made them who they were.

A small irritant continued to niggle at her. Their clothes were strewn from the front door to the bedroom, carelessly dropped where they'd been removed. She couldn't remember the last time she'd gone to bed without putting her things away. A lifetime of discipline, and where had it gotten her?

Habits formed in life had kept her apartment neat as a pin, her CDs in alphabetical order, her shoes arranged by style and color. But it was a place she'd inhabited alone. Discipline at work had kept her devoted to a job for years that was lost in the blink of an eye. Of course, without the regimentation she wouldn't have risen to the position she'd held, wouldn't have gone to that office party or worn a stunning gown that caught the attention of a sexy, handsome model.

Steven hummed in his sleep, rolled over and pulled her against him. "Yes, indeed," she whispered, "just *look* where discipline's gotten me."

She closed her eyes and fell asleep.

* * * *

"Gramps, I wouldn't say that spell was very successful." Edwina turned from the front window where she'd watched Derica snuggle against Kailen.

"You wouldn't, my dear? Why ever not?" Nigel raised his brows at his granddaughter.

"Well, usually we disappear after the first visit. Derica had to come in twice in order for things to work out." She frowned. "Didn't I do the dress right?"

Nigel leaned back against the counter and crossed his arms. "You did the spell perfectly, Edwina. You're learning so fast. The dress was to get Derica in the photo shoot. The package was to get her to see that Steven loved her. If not for the mix-up in packages, they might have stumbled through more weeks of not knowing how the other felt, and it's time they move on and start having little ones."

"So sometimes a second zap is necessary?"

His moustache twitched. Straightening to his full height he looked down at her with a stern expression. "We do not '*zap*,' Edwina, we nudge. It's up to the humans to follow where we nudge, but that's all we do. And yes, sometimes it takes more than once."

Her smile brought a corresponding smile to her grandfather's face. "Okay, I think I see now." Happy, she moved to the back of the store. "I think I'll make us some tea. And maybe we have some of that bread left, and some blackberry jam. Where are we going next?"

Nigel followed Edwina. "Tea and bread sounds very good, my dear. And we're going to Virginia. Have you been with me to Virginia before?"

"No, I don't think so."

"Well, you'll like it. The mountains are soft and covered in trees, and there're pockets of mystery and magic left there from the old days, when the hills were young."

"Hmm, sounds lovely."

"It is, as you will see."

Awards Night

Dee S. Knight

Chapter One

Allison Hayes berated herself for the millionth time as she hurried up the street. Spending her lunch hour shopping wasn't her greatest desire, but she had little choice.

Why had she agreed to help at the reunion yet again? Hadn't she been masochistic enough when they'd celebrated being out of high school five years? She'd handled all of the arrangements then. And when the tenth anniversary arrived, hadn't she accepted the tasks of tracking down everyone in their class, bringing in the entertainment and setting up the welcome dinner?

As the third reunion approached, she'd determined to stay out of it. Yet here she was, sucked in again. At least this time she only had responsibility for handling the welcome table for the mix-and-mingle dinner on Saturday. The opening ceremonies, as it were.

"And I think that will be the extent of my appearances, too," she mumbled. Why emphasize the chasm that existed between her and her classmates one more time?

The first reunion hadn't been so bad in that respect. Everyone either had recently graduated from college or was trying to establish their place in the world in some way. She'd felt on equal footing. At the next, she had been among the few who weren't married, one of only a handful who hadn't left the Lexington area. This year, she knew she would be almost alone in her single status. Probably a few of her classmates had been divorced and remarried, even, sampling two or three times what she hadn't known at all. She would feel odd and provincial, still being unmarried and never having left their small hometown.

Walking with purpose down Main Street, she headed for the Belk's department store. The reunion committee, in its infinite wisdom, had decided to make the introductory party a retro theme.

"So much more fun," her friend Mary had explained on the phone last week.

"Fun? But I don't have anything I can wear to a retro party. I'm not even sure what retro clothes are," Allison had complained.

"Sure you do. Now look, Allison, you *must* be there. I'm really counting on you. It'll be fun, you'll see. Have your hair styled in a flip and find an old bridesmaid's dress somewhere. Somehow they always look like they're from the fifties." With that bit of sage advice she'd hung up to take care of some child-related disaster in the making.

So here Allison was, on her lunch hour and only a few days before the event, trying to find something that filled the requirements. Tugging on the door to Belk's, she saw the sign posted on the glass: "Closed due to broken pipe. Please visit us again later this week."

"Great." Heaving a deep sigh, she wondered where else she could find the kind of dress she needed, in—she glanced at her watch—thirty minutes. Nowhere. She groaned knowing she'd now have to do more shopping than could be handled in a lunch break.

Viewing her reflection in the glass, she noted the lines of fatigue already there, and the week wasn't over yet. Leaving her plain face starkly exposed, her brown hair was pulled back in a bun, its luster normally hidden under a nurse's cap. She looked tidy and efficient in the white uniform. But she hurt from the hours on her feet combined with the walk uptown, making her lean to the right in order to take weight off her left leg. The ache added to her weary expression. The last thing she needed was to go shopping.

"Damn!" She hadn't wanted to go to the reunion in the first place and now she had to rearrange her schedule in order to find a dress she really didn't want to buy. She turned to trudge back up the street toward the hospital.

Suddenly, a noise caught her attention and she glanced up to find the source, a sign hanging over the sidewalk, squeaking on its hinges. *Your Desire*, the sign said in fine script. *Vintage Clothing.* An arrow pointed up the alley where Allison saw another, smaller sign hanging over a doorway. Puzzled, she looked up and down the street. She'd never noticed this sign before. She hadn't especially noticed this alley, to tell the truth. *Vintage Clothing.*

"What do I have to lose?" she murmured, dragging herself up the alleyway.

Pushing open the door, she experienced a rush of anticipation, a tingle up her spine. She walked into a store surprisingly different than what she'd expected. From the outside, the storefront appeared tiny. Inside, shelves and racks spaced on each wall extended far into the back, making the shop very deep. She supposed because the windows fronted the alley, the natural light that filled the space seemed filtered, creating a hazy, gauzy ambience.

She stepped farther inside. Background music was loud enough to be heard but not overwhelming. A song by a swing band ended and a Hit

Parade ballad by Perry Como began. To her left she saw a Victorian wedding gown hanging on the wall. To her right, a flapper era dress, complete with fringe and sequins. Surely these were reproductions. No one store could have such a wide range of exquisite originals.

"May I help you?"

She started, slapping her hand to her chest. "Oh, I didn't see you." The man standing beside her looked like someone she thought she should know. An actor or something. That was it! One of those old actors. What was his name…?

He smiled and she forgot to remember.

"I didn't mean to startle you. Are you looking for something in particular?"

"Yes," she said, regaining her composure. "I need a dress for an event on Saturday. Do you carry anything fifties-like?"

"We certainly do, and I might have something in your size. Let's see…." He cast a glance over her while tapping his lips with his index finger. "I believe you look about a size twelve?"

"You have a good eye."

He smiled again. "Years of experience, my dear. Come this way."

His walk was so smooth he almost seemed to glide across the floor. Following, Allison's limp was even more pronounced. The ache in her hip had spread to her lower back and finishing her shift would be hell.

When the man stopped in front of a rack of dresses, she saw clothing from the right era. A gray poodle skirt and pink sweater set were displayed on a mannequin with bright, rosy cheeks and a long ponytail streaked with pink and green. Then the mannequin moved.

"This is my granddaughter, Edwina," the man said by way of introduction. "And I do apologize. I'm Nigel Brown. May I have your name?"

"Allison Hayes."

"Of course." His eyes twinkled but not in merriment. More like in confirmation. Then he turned to his granddaughter. "Edwina, would you show Miss Hayes what we have from the fifties? The dress is for a dance, I believe?" He raised his brows.

"More like a cocktail party-slash-dinner. For a high school reunion."

"Oh, what fun," Edwina said, smiling.

Not! "I hope so."

"Now, Miss Hayes, why don't you just have a seat and we'll show you what we have. I'm certain we can find something magical for you." He pointed to a chair Allison was fairly certain had not been there a short minute ago, and she gladly sank onto the seat.

"Not magical, Mr. Brown. I don't believe in magic, I'm afraid. Just something to fit the theme so I can get through the evening."

"We'll just see, shall we?" He winked at her.

For the next ten minutes Edwina held up dresses, more for her grandfather's inspection than Allison's. He found something wrong with each one before Allison could voice an opinion. The gorgeous red chiffon was *too* red for her coloring, the white velvet, too small. An adorable satin jacket dress in lavender was too large and a strapless brocade, too old. "Edwina, *really*," he'd said dramatically.

133

"This is the last we have, Gramps." Screwing her face up in distaste, Edwina held up a ball length gown. Allison knew her mouth fell open as she examined the garment.

Gold, brown and dark green plaid. It was plaid *taffeta*. The skirt was overly full. Two straps extended from the sleeveless bodice to tie behind the wearer's neck.

Nigel Brown cocked his head and a slow smile spread across his face. "Yes," he murmured, as though to himself. "She's an autumn, and these are the perfect colors for her. The size is exact—she won't even have to try it on." Beaming, he turned to Allison. "Didn't I tell you we'd find exactly the right thing, my dear?"

She tried to keep horror from showing on her face. "But-but, Mr. Brown, this dress is….um…"

"Hideous?" Edwina supplied.

"Yes," Allison grasped at the word. "Yes, it's hideous. You can't possibly think I should wear *this* to my reunion." Her voice tapered to a whisper. "Can you?"

He stared at her with that same knowing smile and patted her shoulder. "You're looking at the gown on the hanger. Most clothes aren't at their best when they're hanging up. They need the human form to give them character. And this dress will show real character on you, Allison. You can trust me."

Standing, she walked to Edwina, who pursed her lips and raised her brows, openly showing the skepticism Allison wanted to show, but was too polite. Taking a piece of material in her hand, she stretched her arm to shoulder height. Volumes of material still fell in folds from the hanger.

"Mr. Brown, there's so much here. *Too* much, and...*plaid*. You *do* see, don't you? I can't possibly wear this."

Edwina heaved a sigh and looked to her grandfather.

"Allison," his voice fell, became smoother, melodious.

Allison blinked, dropped the material and focused hard to hear him.

"This dress is the right time period, the right size, and absolutely right for *you*. You want this dress, you're just not used to the style or the color. When you prepare for your evening, you'll feel like a queen. Your world will change, like magic. I promise you."

"You do?" A queen. Such a change would *take* magic, for she'd never felt like a queen. Well, maybe before the accident she'd been made to feel like a *princess*, but she'd been nine when the horse threw her, so that hardly counted.

"I do," he confirmed. "Now, shall we wrap this up for you?"

"Yes, please."

He smiled happily. "Oh, I'm so glad, my dear. You won't regret this purchase. I can see you now, dancing across the floor"—he waved his arms through the air as though guiding someone in a waltz—"the skirt billowing behind you and the crinkle of taffeta emphasizing every graceful turn. You'll be smashing!"

She hadn't noticed Edwina slipping away but when Allison turned, she saw the girl at the back of the store, putting the dress in a box. She hurried to the counter. "How much is it? I didn't even look at the price."

"Thirty dollars. Does that seem too much?" Edwina sounded as though she thought any amount would be too much.

"Are you kidding? It's far too little. I mean, this truly has to be vintage—surely no one would make a dress like this anymore."

Edwina coughed out a laugh. "That's true, surely no one would. Nonetheless, that's what we're charging."

Allison looked for Nigel. He stood where she'd left him, watching her. "Mr. Brown? Are you certain of this price?"

"You really are a good woman, Allison. Thirty dollars, please, and you let us worry about our profit margin, all right?"

Shrugging, she dug out her wallet. "All right, I guess. Thank you very much." Handing Edwina the money with one hand, she accepted the box with the other. "Well, if I ever need something old-fashioned again, I'll be back."

"Oh, I don't imagine you'll need us again," Nigel said, suddenly standing beside her. He frowned. "Hold still, my dear. You have a piece of lint in your hair." He reached his hand to her, letting his fingers linger briefly on her forehead. Warmth spread outward from his touch. The area around her hip and back felt hot. Her pain diminished and then petered out.

She felt her eyes widen in surprise. Twisting from side to side, she waited for the customary spasms to set her nerve endings afire, but nothing happened. "How did you—"

"There, I think I got it." He held out his fingers, but she didn't see anything.

Then it didn't seem important that she know how the pain had disappeared. Smiling at the two shopkeepers, she said, "Thanks. I'd better go now."

"Have a good time at your event," Nigel called as she went out the door.

With renewed vigor, she walked to the top of the alley and turned toward the hospital, certain she was late. Glancing at her watch, she was astounded to see that only a few minutes had passed from when she'd left Belk's. *Belk's?*

She spun around, confused. A woman outside Belk's pulled open the door and entered the department store. Another, holding a shopping bag with one hand and a child with the other, came out.

But I didn't go into Belk's—did I? Frowning, she looked at the mouth of the alley. *There had been a sign, advertising a shop of some kind.* No sign hung there now.

However, there was definitely a dress box under her arm, marked Your Desire. A moment's unease struck, then faded to nothing. There was no place along the street except the chain department store where she could have gotten a dress.

Your Desire must be a new line at Belk's, she told herself, at the same time marveling at how good she felt. With an actual spring in her step, she headed back to work.

* * * *

I was the laughingstock of the evening.

So went Allison's thoughts as she drove the twisty road between town and her farm. She would never understand how she'd come to buy the dress she was wearing. The thing was horrid, awful, *hideous*. Yes. That was the perfect description.

Strangely, when she'd gotten dressed for the evening, she hadn't thought she looked hideous at all. In fact, when she finished dressing, with her hair curled and held softly off her face with satin-finish gold barrettes, and light touches of makeup applied, she'd examined herself critically in the full-length mirror. A smile had touched her lips and her eyes. She looked fine, she thought. In fact, she'd shyly admitted to herself, she felt just like Cinderella going off to the royal dance. Twirling, pretending she was in the arms of her Prince Charming, she'd closed her eyes, loving the feel of the stiff fabric as it moved, and the sound of the taffeta swishing around her legs.

Tossing the end of a wool shawl over one shoulder, she'd confidently walked to her car and driven to the landmark hotel in town, where the evening's activities were taking place.

The first hint something was wrong was the look on Mary's face. The two friends hadn't found time to speak earlier, so when she arrived Mary rushed to give her a hug. Then she'd stepped back and examined Allison.

"I love the way you've done your hair," she'd finally said.

"Thanks." Allison gave a hesitant smile, then twirled for Mary as she had for herself earlier that evening. *Swish, crinkle, swish* went the skirt. "What do you think? Isn't the dress something?"

"Yesss, it is. Nice… I like the shawl very much."

Allison's smile disappeared. She took in the concerned look on Mary's face. *Her* appearance was perfect. Long blond hair curled charmingly over her shoulders. The floor-length gown, white, scattered with sprigs of lavender-colored flowers, was a shirt-waist style with a short jacket to match. All of that, plus a petite frame and face with laughing blue eyes, made her the very picture of a young starlet from 1955, instead of the thirty-something widow and mother of two she actually was.

Even in her normal role, Mary was beautiful and graceful, the opposite of Allison. Despite her self-consciously unfavorable comparison to her friend, she and Mary had always been close.

"Oh dear, Mary. My outfit seemed just right when I got it. Do you really think it's awful?" She held out her skirt and looked down, frowning.

"No, no, of course it's not awful. Don't pay any attention to me, Allison. The dress is fine. There's just so much to it and the color is a little dark. Reminds me of autumn in Scotland instead of spring in Virginia. Actually"—she took a longer look at the dress, frowning in her examination—"it reminds me of that autumn I spent in Scotland after college, sampling Guinness at every pub I came to. This is the way a good many mornings looked to me." Shaking her head at the memory, she took Allison's hand. "I'm sorry. Don't worry, really, the dress is fine. Come on. Let me show you the table and what I'd like you to do."

That began the evening. Before long, she'd endured enough long stares and quick embarrassed glances to last a lifetime. Although Mary had insisted that Allison sit at her table for dinner and drinks, when the nametags had been handed out and the hellos said, Allison slipped out and headed home.

Twenty minutes later she turned from the dark county road onto her long driveway. The headlights swept the fence and pastureland as she made the turn, catching something out of place in their beams. She stopped and backed up. A man was rising from where he'd been sitting in her pasture. Not far away, the bumper of a light-colored sports car had made a good-sized dent in one of her oak trees.

"Good Lord!" She jumped out. "Mister! Mister, can you hear me? Are you all right?"

He faced her, looking dazed but uninjured, from what she could see. He made no attempt to move toward her. "Hello? I've had an accident."

"Yes, I can see that." When he still made no effort to move toward her, she got a flashlight from the glove box, heaved a sigh of resignation and gathered up the volume of skirt so she could climb the wooden fence, grateful for once that she was unable to wear heels. Then she cringed when she thought of how her beautiful velvet slippers would look by the time she trudged across the wet grass. They'd look like hell, and so would the bottom half of her dress.

"'Like hell' can only be an improvement on the dress," she muttered.

Even with the flashlight, the headlights cast eerie shadows in front of her as she carefully picked her way across the wet, ankle high grass. Despite the dew-soaked hem, she sounded like an army of taffeta-clothed soldiers crossing the field. In the quiet, the scratchy, swishy noise of the stiff material rang through the night. Except for the sound of the car engine, her dress made the only noise, since the man had said nothing else

"Are you *hurt?*" she asked when she reached him.

A glance to the left showed a gaping hole in the fence that would have to be repaired very quickly. Lucky the sheep are in the lower pasture, she thought, then chastised herself for thinking about her sheep when something was clearly wrong with the man standing in front of her. The very *handsome* man, even with the sharp angles and dark shadows on his face cast by the unnatural lighting.

"Who are you?" he asked sharply.

His tone pierced her romantic examination of his face and raised her hackles. After the night she'd already had there was no way she felt like putting up with rudeness, even rudeness due to shock.

"I'm the owner of the fence you smashed through and the tree whose trunk you gouged. Now would you mind answering my question? I'm also a nurse. I want to know if I should call 911 for an ambulance or only call the police."

He looked like he was considering her statement.

"Is your car drivable? It doesn't look too bad, actually, from what I can see. Better than my tree."

"I don't know. I didn't try."

"Well, at least you didn't back up through the huge hole you put in my fence and drive off without a leaving me a note or anything. I appreciate that." She looked him over as well as she could. No blood that she could see. He was standing and didn't show signs of being in pain, or dizzy. His color was pretty good. So, what didn't seem right?

141

"You don't *look* hurt. Come on up to the house. I'll get your insurance information and we can report this to the police." She hesitated. "You haven't been drinking, have you? Because things will go a lot worse for you if you have."

"No, I haven't been drinking."

"Okay, good. Come on, then." She turned and marched back toward the car. *Swish, crinkle, scratch, swish.*

"Wait."

She realized he wasn't following when he called. "What?" she said, sounding only slightly less exasperated than she felt.

"I can't follow you." He roughly raked his hand through his hair and grimaced. Dropping his arm, he blew out a harsh breath. "I can't see."

Your Desire

Dee S. Knight

Chapter Two

She must have run back toward him. He didn't know exactly what made that rustling sound, but he was happy for it. The sound meant a person was here, not whatever made the kinds of noises he'd been listening to for the past hour or more. And this person was someone who seemed to have a level head and didn't panic easily, thank God, because inside he felt panicked enough for both of them.

Her hand grasped his arm. "You can't see at all? Anything?"

He shook his head.

"Not even this?"

"No, I told you." What was she doing, waving a red flag in front of his face? "Do you think if I could see I'd be sitting here on wet grass, freezing to death, waiting for a woman who can't understand English well enough to know what I mean when I say I can't see anything?"

Damn it! His voice, rising in volume with each word, clearly betrayed the terror he didn't want known. It had been years since he'd allowed himself any kind of unchecked emotion. In fact, this display was so atypical he felt a thread of surprise twisting through the fear. The emotional reaction was only as unusual as the situation, however. He'd never been so totally out of control and helpless.

To her credit, the woman didn't react to his voice or words. Not that he could tell anyway. She didn't remove her hand from his arm and when she spoke her voice was firm and untainted by sarcasm or hurt feelings.

"Okay, I understand. I can't examine you well enough out here. Can you walk if I lead you?"

"Yes." His heart was pounding. He hated feeling weak. Hated appearing weak even more.

"Good." She rustled from in front of him to his side and took his hand.

"Wait. Can you get something out of the car?" Hearing her quick exhalation indicating impatience, he added, "It's my wallet."

"Okay."

"And my briefcase and cell phone," he said in a rush.

"Anything else?" Her tone dripped honey. "I mean, I have a strong back if you'd like me to strap on your luggage."

Fine. After all he'd been through, this is just what he needed. "Thank you, no. The things I listed would cause a great deal of trouble if something happened to the car. I really need them." Whereas her words had been honeyed sarcasm, he knew his were unemotional and cold. He'd used the tone often enough in business to have it perfected.

"Okay. Wait here." Without a word, she dropped his hand. *Swish, swish.* The sound moved away. "Where are they? I don't see anything here."

"The phone should be on the console between the front seats. The briefcase is in the trunk and my wallet is in the glove box. Oh, and my jacket is on the backseat." He heard her talking. "What? I can't hear you."

"First you can't see and now you can't hear," she grumbled as she swished up. "What I was saying wasn't for your shell-like ears, believe me." Firmly, she grabbed his wrist and extended his arm, turning his palm up to slap two objects in it. "Here's your phone, which was under the seat, and your wallet." She draped something over his arm. "Your jacket was jumbled up on the floor. How do I get into the trunk?"

"Oh, right." He dug in his pocket and came up with keys. "Use the long one." She snatched them out of his hand and crinkled away again.

A click indicated the trunk opened. "Ouch, damn it!" indicated a rapid approach to the proverbial end of the rope for the woman. She confirmed his theory when she returned after slamming the trunk lid harder than it had ever been slammed in the years he'd owned the car.

"That's enough. We're going to get you to the hospital now. No more fetch and carry, no more discussion. Unless," she added, "you'd just like to sit out here the rest of the night."

That was no question and he had no choice.

"Thank you. I appreciate your help. Did you hit your head on the trunk lid?" He let the concern he felt infuse his voice. This woman was helping him. Nastiness wasn't called for, considering how much he needed her.

She'd taken his hand again and started walking haltingly, waiting for him with each step. Gingerly putting his foot out and patting the ground before stepping forward, it felt like each bit of progress took minutes.

"Yes." She didn't sound upset anymore.

She'd taken so long to answer, he had to remind himself what the response was for. So she *had* hit her head. "I'm sorry." If her head was as lovely as her voice, he truly *was* sorry.

147

Talking would have taken his mind off his situation. He needed to think to talk effectively. Not walking, though. Walking, after all, was an associative action, not cognitive. He walked all the time without having to think about how. In fact, frequently he walked and carried on multiple, simultaneous conversations. No big deal.

This was different, though, and the knowledge that he couldn't walk without almost total concentration on his feet and where to place them brought back the fear he'd temporarily forgotten. The helplessness that accompanied the blindness threatened to engulf him if he didn't concentrate on something. Fortunately, the "something" was taking tiny steps toward her car, which she'd left running. Engine noise had never sounded so good.

"It's okay," she finally answered. "I apologize for my language. I was more frustrated than hurt. Why were you sitting on the ground instead of in the car?"

At that moment, his foot struck a rock protruding from the ground and he stumbled. Only her steadying hold and unexpected strength kept him from falling to his knees.

"Steady." She soothed him with her soft drawl. "We're almost to the fence." The rustle was less noticeable with their slow movement, but the sound still calmed him, almost as much as her voice and solid grip.

"After the accident I think I blacked out. When I opened my eyes, I thought I was just stunned when I couldn't see. Then I imagined the smell of gasoline and I heard a hissing from under the hood. I didn't know if the car might catch fire or explode, so I got out and tried to move away from it."

"Cars don't normally explode after accidents. That's just on TV and the movies." She sounded as though she were lecturing a child.

"Easy for you to say. I know that, of course, but you weren't there, blind and disoriented. I had no idea what was going on around me." In his petulance he started to pull away from her, but she held him tightly.

"I know, I know. I'm sorry. I didn't mean to hurt your tender feelings. Your hands are freezing cold. I'd have thought you'd sit inside the car where it was dry and warmer. What if I hadn't come home early? You could have been out there for hours."

"Huh." The grunt didn't begin to express the distaste he felt for that thought, or the gratitude to the gods who had brought her home from wherever she'd been, ahead of time.

"If you haven't been drinking, why'd you run through my fence?"

"Jesus, that fence again. You'd've thought I hit it on purpose."

"Stop! Move to the left a little. Okay," she said after they made the adjustment. "The ground was a little uneven there. Not too much farther now."

He had to hand it to her. Now that they were actually in action, she was unflappable. He wished he didn't feel like such a weakling. Then he wouldn't sound like such a prick.

"A deer."

"What?"

"A deer ran out in front of me." He hesitated. "I might have been going a little too fast and it was getting dark."

"I see."

"I'll pay for the fence."

"Yes, you will." There was no heat in her tone, she was simply making a statement. "There are thousands of deer out here. You're lucky you weren't hurt." They didn't slow down but he could sense her mentally stopping and evaluating him. "You *were* blinded in the *accident*, right? I mean, you weren't driving around out here blind, were you?"

She sounded amused and he laughed in response. God, it felt wonderful to laugh at something.

"Good." The satisfaction in her voice was a balm.

Well, hell. She'd *tried* to make him laugh, to let him know he was going to be okay and could loosen up.

Some of the tension drained from him. Unaccustomed as he was to feeling dependent, he knew without doubt this woman was someone he could trust with his fear. She wouldn't judge him harshly for a moment of dependence.

"Okay, we're at the fence. It's wooden and two-railed." She placed his hands on the top rail and released him. "Let me put the flashlight and briefcase down, then get on the other side, and then—"

A sound like crinkling plastic bags filled the night. A soft thud signaled her landing on the other side of the fence. Suddenly she stood directly in front of him, her breath hot on his neck in the cool night air, her hand brushing his temple so gently the touch might have been the wings of a moth. Lifting his hand to place over hers, he gave himself over to the sensation of tenderness. For just a minute he released concern, allowing himself to draw succor from her.

Even though he could see nothing with his eyes open, he closed them. As improbable as the event seemed, standing in an open pasture, blinded and half in shock, his cock rose at her touch. He didn't fight his reaction to her, he welcomed it. This was a sign of normalcy in the otherwise fantastic events and emotions of the evening.

He couldn't see this woman, didn't know the feel of her hard nipples crushed against his chest or the sound of her moan as her tight muscles gripped his cock and milked him with her orgasm, but for a moment he experienced the security and contentment he somehow knew he would find buried to the hilt in her wet heat. It was all he could do to keep from gasping with pleasure.

Her thumb stroked across his eyebrow. "I don't even know your name." Her voice was as soft as her touch.

He became harder yet, wanting this calm, dependable woman more than he had ever wanted anyone else. Only a second is what he took to consider what to tell her. His real name, not the one he used for business. "Frank. Frank Hughes. What about you?"

"Allison Hayes."

He heard a sigh escape her. He'd only just formed the thought of pulling her to him for a kiss when she was all business again.

"Now, Frank, the first rail is about two feet from the ground. Step up then swing your right leg over. Without your sight you might feel a little disoriented, but I'm here to steady you."

She was right. With her hands bracing his arm and side, and her encouraging noises in his ear, he easily made it over the fence. But even doing something so simple made him slightly dizzy. Plus, his head had begun to ache.

Wasting no more time, she bundled him into the car. They backed up and she took off, like the devil himself was chasing them.

* * * *

Within minutes of arriving at the trauma center, Frank was fitted with a neck brace by a brisk and efficient nurse. She exchanged a few words of greeting with Allison before firing triage questions regarding the nature of the accident and the condition in which Allison had found him. For his part, he gave terse, firm answers, showing no sign of the nervousness his grip transmitted since first taking Allison's hand when they entered the building. She couldn't help but admire his control.

Before he could articulate an argument, Allison forced her hand from his to help the nurse remove his shirt. He sputtered protests as they slipped a hospital gown over his shoulders. Allison tied it in the back while the nurse removed the rest of his clothing, amidst louder protests.

"Nothing I haven't seen before, Mr. Hughes, no need to worry." Her voice was soothing, but she sent a thumbs up and a smile to Allison over his shoulder. "Let's get you to radiology." Settling him on the bed, she released the wheel brakes and pushed.

"Wait a minute!" Frank commanded.

The nurse slowed but didn't stop.

"Allison, you're coming with me."

Briefly, she bristled at his presumptuousness. But one look at his white-knuckled fists lying on the sheet told her what she needed to do. "Yes, I'm right with you, Frank," she replied in a low voice, and they set off through the labyrinth of hallways.

Allison sighed at the number of people waiting in the radiology area. Saturday nights, even in small towns, always produced business for hospitals. The fact that there was a line didn't matter, however. Concern over his possible injuries was great enough that Frank was wheeled in ahead of everyone else.

"You'll be fine," Allison said, patting his shoulder. "I'll wait here for you."

He opened his mouth to say something, but the nurse gave him no chance, pushing him through the doors as he sputtered. Stifling a laugh, Allison found a chair and dropped into it. She wished she had someplace to prop her feet and relieve the pressure on her legs.

Across the room, a small boy stared at her, stubby fingers jammed in his mouth. She smiled and wiggled her fingers. He widened his eyes, opened his mouth and emitted a wail that made everyone wince.

Great. Just what she needed. Thankfully, his mother picked him up, shooting a dirty look at Allison as she did.

Several minutes later, a different nurse emerged with Frank to return him to the emergency room. After locking the bed in place, she bustled about, murmuring words of comfort and encouragement. She tucked the sheet around him, then cursed under her breath when he sat and upset her efforts.

"Lie down, please, Mr. Hughes."

"I don't want to lie down," he growled. His emotional control showed signs of failing.

Grasping his arms to push him back, she replied, "You *must* lie down."

"No." Like a stubborn boy, he set his lips. "I have phone calls to make. It's uncomfortable talking on the phone when I'm reclined. Go away."

She let go of him and looked at Allison who shook her head as though to say she didn't know how to handle him either.

"Allison?" No growl now, but he definitely didn't sound happy.

"Yes, Frank." She moved forward.

"I don't want to lie down. Will you explain that to her, nurse to nurse?"

"Frank, please lie back. You'll feel better if you do. I promise I won't leave. Okay?"

Mumbling things she was sure she should be glad not to hear, he nonetheless lay back on the bed.

Allison looked at the nurse. "I'll take care of him."

"Thanks. He's all yours." She left, letting the curtain fall closed behind her.

"You're lucky, Frank. Mike Beam is on duty tonight and he's the best trauma doctor in the county."

"Thanks, Allison." A tall, slender man in his mid-fifties strode into the curtained cubicle, carrying a medical chart he read as he walked.

She flashed the doctor a welcoming smile. "Hi, Mike. This is Frank Hughes. His car crashed in my front pasture and he hasn't been able to see since then."

"All right, Mr. Hughes, let's take a look."

Allison removed her hand from Frank's then stepped back from the table.

"You're not leaving are you?" he asked.

"I'll stay if you want me to."

"Yes." The word was a command, but there was a note of relief beneath it.

Mike removed the brace and then peered into Frank's eyes. With the surety of a skilled healer, he checked Frank's head, neck and shoulders carefully for any signs of injury or pain. The grimace she'd seen in the pasture when Frank ran his hand through his hair, marked his face again when Mike touched the back of his head and neck. Fortunately, there were no cuts or abrasions.

"I've looked at the X-rays and didn't see anything broken. I'd like to do an MRI, then we'll know more," Mike said, noting the orders on the chart. "Right now, I'll take a chance and say the diagnosis is contusion and blindness caused by trauma. I'd bet that when you had your accident, your head went forward and snapped back against the headrest, causing swelling of the brain in the area dealing with sight. That's back here." He lightly touched the back of Frank's head. "If we don't see anything else in the MRI we'll go with that. And I'll ask Walt Neeley and Dick Matthews to take a look, too."

"Who're they?" With the doctor, his voice was once again firm, controlling, taking no prisoners.

"The staff ophthalmologist and neurologist. In these cases, once the swelling goes down, sight usually comes back."

"How long?"

"Hard to say. Healing could take a few days or a few weeks."

"Weeks! I can't be away from my business—"

"Don't get all excited. Tests first. I'll send someone to take you down." He started to exit and then stopped, turning to Allison with a puzzled smile. "I thought you had a reunion to attend tonight? How did you end up at home so early?" He glanced at the chart. "This shows you were here before nine o'clock."

She gave a non-committal shrug. "I was there for a little while but didn't feel like hanging around." Mike and his wife were good friends and knew how little she socialized. As much as she sometimes wanted to go out for fun, she usually felt more at ease sharing her free time with the kids in the county's literacy program or volunteering at the battered women's shelter. They had lectured her frequently about the need for relaxing, personal time.

"Ah." There seemed to be a world behind that one word. Not even a word, more a sound. Then he quirked his brows, shrugged and gave a sigh of resignation that meant he knew he couldn't change her. "Interesting dress." Another world of hidden meaning.

"I like that dress," Frank interjected with a force that surprised her. She stepped forward to rest her hand on his arm. Vibrations of power surrounded him like an aura, yet there on the table, in the cold blaze of hospital lights, he looked like a man who desperately needed a simple touch.

"Yes, well, you're blind." Mike winked at her as he left.

"What did he mean by that?" demanded Frank.

"Never mind." She leaned closer to say, "The man has no taste. You should see the tie he's wearing."

He chuckled warmly as a nurse tore back the curtain and marched in, followed by an orderly pushing a gurney.

"Hi, Allison. What did you find in your front yard?"

"Linda, how's it going?"

"Busy as usual for a Saturday. Okay, Mr. Hughes, take it easy and just let us do the work here." Smoothly, they transferred him from the bed to the gurney. Linda draped a sheet over him, tucking in the edges. "We're just going to the adjoining building for your MRI. It's a simple procedure, but will take a little while. Then I'll bring you back here."

"Allison, aren't you coming with me?" His face puckered into a frown even as Linda and the orderly pushed him out of the cubicle and whisked him down the corridor.

"I'll wait here," Allison called.

She rubbed her face, suddenly very tired. Instead of settling in the chair, she headed for the nurses' lounge. Her wet slippers made a sad, uneven plopping sound as she crept down the hall, her tiredness making her limp more pronounced.

With a cup of coffee that tasted and smelled like it'd been boiled twice, she sank onto the cushioned loveseat and lifted her feet to the rickety coffee table. The events of the night had been truly remarkable, starting with the horrid reunion and ending with finding a fantastic man practically in her front yard.

Frank was obviously somebody. His clothing wasn't inexpensive and his fingernails were manicured, not the norm for the men she usually encountered. He had the confidence of a sophisticated man who knew he held power. Unlike anyone she'd ever been attracted to, there was certainly an allure about him that pulled her, called her. She'd wanted him to kiss her when they stood at the fence. If he hadn't been injured and in need of her professionalism, she might have kissed him.

No, probably not.

She'd wanted to, though.

Closing her eyes, she let her mind drift. Suddenly, she wasn't wearing her noisy, ugly dress. She wore a gown light as air and silky soft, and she was naked beneath. Even without a mirror for confirmation, she knew she was beautiful, with no scars or limp. She floated across the floor, as the man in the store had. In her dream she frowned slightly, trying to remember the man, but her frown faded when she saw Frank.

In a blink, like events happen in dreams, they were naked. His cock was breathtaking in size, hard and erect.

"For you," he whispered. "Only for you."

"Yes, please." She lay back and spread her legs. His lips seared a path of kisses up the inside of her leg. His tongue bathed her clit, while fingers probed her inner depths.

Then his tongue swirled around her nipple and she felt the initial tap of his cock against her vagina. A slight nudge is all it took, she was so wet. Already she smelled the powerful scent of their combined arousal.

"Allison, I can't wait any longer." With a hard push, he drove into her. The stroke robbed her of breath, but she wrapped him with her legs and arms and rose to meet him—

"He wants you, you know."

The voice came from far off, but it wasn't in her dream. This was real.

"Allison?"

She jerked upright, narrowly preventing the spill of tepid coffee in her lap. "What? Who?"

"The impatient patient. He demanded someone find you, and here I am, finding you." Pushing the door further open, Linda leaned her shoulder against the jamb while Allison put her feet on the floor and rubbed her eyes in an effort to wake up.

Linda looked at her with some amusement. "He's quite a hunk and seems to have developed an attachment to you. Got a bear of a personality when you're not around, and is a pussy cat when you are. Are you sure you just met this guy?"

Allison laughed. "Just tonight. You could say we met by accident." Studying her friend she added, "Don't you want to say something about my dress? This lovely gown was the hit of my reunion." She tossed her Styrofoam cup in the trash can and walked back toward the ER with Linda.

"That's right, your reunion *was* tonight. I hate those things, myself. My tenth is coming up next year." Linda stopped and shot Allison a calculated look. "Tell me the truth, do I look like I've gained weight in the past few years?"

Truthfully, she did appear to have put on about fifteen pounds or so. "Not an ounce," Allison said firmly.

Linda nodded, satisfaction spreading across her face. "Thanks, you're a pal. And in the same vein of honesty, I think your dress is beautiful."

Smiling, Allison left Linda at the nurses' station and made her way along the wall of curtained off areas.

* * * *

"Where is the damn doctor?" His truculent tone was understandable but wearying just the same, after an hour of waiting for test results.

A fair portion of that time he'd spent talking via cell phone to someone named David. That's all she'd heard of the conversations, except Frank's tone, which was commanding. He was definitely a man used to giving orders.

Evidently David could also give a few. When she'd checked at the desk to ask what else needed to be done in the way of paperwork for admission, the clerk had told her everything was being handled. Not only had the tedious forms been taken care of and insurance approved, the X-ray and MRI results were being sent to Frank's doctor's computer in Washington so he could consult on treatment.

"The doctor will be here as soon as he knows something." She gave him her best grim nurse's look before remembering he couldn't see her expression. Instead she patted his hand as though he were a child. "Stop being a baby. Everything that can be done is being done."

Three different doctors had examined him in the time they'd been at the hospital, coming in, saying as little as possible, then leaving with a "Hmm." She knew it was the lack of information that grated on Frank's nerves more than anything else.

While the doctors checked him over, she'd examined him herself, with as little notice as possible. He was as handsome as any man she'd ever seen, but in a rugged way, contrary to the citified, expensive clothes he wore. There was a bump at the top of his nose indicating at least one break. Long luxurious lashes swept down and up each time he blinked, hiding then revealing beautiful hazel eyes. He was tall and very fit, muscled without an ounce of fat. Brown hair, nicely trimmed, sparkled with good health and care. In the bright glare of ER lights, his face didn't look nearly so sharply angled as she'd thought earlier, but the stubble from a day's growth of beard made him look dark and rough.

"Tell you what. Why don't I go and get you some ice? You shouldn't have anything to eat, but a little ice will be all right."

"Ice?" He said it as though he couldn't believe anyone in their right mind would suggest such a thing, but in the end he agreed.

Ten minutes later, she approached his cubicle with a cup filled with shaved ice. Weariness dragged at her with every step, and she could hardly wait until Frank was admitted so she could go home.

"Here comes Allison now. We'll ask her." His voice was loud enough to be heard throughout the ER. She slipped through the opening to see Frank sitting on the edge of the bed. Walter Neeley, the ophthalmologist, stood in front of him. Mike stood apart, his arms crossed over the metal cover of the hospital chart held tightly against his chest. His face was serious but a look of mischievous glee colored his eyes as he observed the verbal sparring between the two men. Beside him stood Richard Matthews, head of neurology, who nodded a greeting to her.

"Ask Allison what?" She knew she'd have to referee something, based on the bull-headed expressions of both doctor and patient. Frank and Walt had already turned toward the opening in the curtains when she slipped in. *This damn noisy dress.*

"I want to hold Mr. Hughes overnight. He refuses. Says he'll be all right at your house." Walt Neeley arched a brow at her. "As he's *your* friend, perhaps you can convince him that it's in his own best interests to be admitted for the night."

Unconsciously, she moved to stand beside Frank, touching his hand to let him know she was there. His head followed her every movement. "Actually he's not my fr—"

"Tell him there's no need for me to remain here overnight, Allison. If he'd give me something for this damn headache, I'd be fine. Well, if I could see, that is." He practically growled out the last.

"They can't give you anything that will make you sleep."

"But it hurts like hell."

"I know, but buck up," she stage-whispered.

He snorted and turned away.

"Actually, Frank," she stated in her most persuasive tone, "it *is* in your best interest to stay here. If anything should happen, the staff and equipment you need will be here."

"No."

Damn it! She couldn't take him home. Besides the obvious medical risks, there was the unsettled feeling she experienced around him. It was unreasonable, but there, nonetheless. Why wouldn't the obstinate man allow them to admit him so she could go home alone to her safe and ordered life.

"Mr. Hughes."

Frank turned his head, his recalcitrant expression carved in stone.

"You don't seem to realize the seriousness of your condition. You have a contusion, and as Nurse Hayes suggested, that's bad enough. But if the swelling of your brain worsens during the night, you'll need care she can't give you at home."

Frank seemed to consider this. "Dr. Matthews, is it?" He asked but continued without waiting for confirmation. "I think I do understand the seriousness of my condition. If you and the staff here haven't explained it thoroughly enough, my own doctor, after examining the test results you sent, has told me plainly that I'm a jackass if I leave here tonight. However, he's well aware of my nature and knows I'm a man used to taking judicious risks. I trust Ms. Hayes. She's a well-trained nurse, is she not?"

"This has nothing to do with Allison's capabilities," spit out Walt Neeley. "This has to do with your welfare and the liability of the hospital if you leave and something happens."

She sighed, knowing the men could butt heads all night without resolution. "What about the blindness?"

Walt spoke. "As far as we can tell, the problem is trauma-induced and will resolve itself when the swelling goes down. Tonight he'll have to be checked every two hours."

"Allison will do that." Frank didn't give the slightest intimation that she might say no.

She looked at him, *really* looked at him. He acted the tyrant, totally commanding, used to having every whim fulfilled and order followed without question. But there was an odd hesitance under it all. She'd noticed the characteristic earlier, too, when they were making their way out of the pasture. Discomfort, almost fear.

His hands fisted on his legs, his brows puckered ever so slightly in worry. Other than those tells, no one would know he wasn't the controlling force he pretended to be. Maybe only she saw he had the false bravado of a man used to being in charge, suddenly finding himself at the mercy of fate. If so, she might not understand his attitude but she wouldn't betray him.

She tried one more approach. "What if I stayed with you? I'd be here each time the nurse woke you up."

He shook his head. "If you won't take me home I'll call my assistant. He'll come down immediately and we'll drive back to DC tonight."

Walt Neeley threw his hands up and snorted in disbelief. Frank's lips turned up in a tiny smile, probably secure in the knowledge that he'd presented an alternative worse than going home with her.

Mike gave a one-shouldered shrug when she glanced at him. "I strongly advise he be admitted." Frank opened his mouth to speak, but Mike cut him off. "If he insists on going, we can't stop him. You're one of the people I'd entrust him to. If you want him, of course."

All four men waited to hear her judgment. "I suppose he could sleep on the sofa in the office. I wouldn't want him climbing the stairs." She spoke out loud, but more to herself, reasoning what to do. "I can get him back here very quickly if need be."

"Good." Frank spoke as though her decision had been a foregone conclusion all along. His hands relaxed on his thighs.

Dr. Matthews slid by on his way out of the cubicle. "You'll have to sign an AMA form. That's Against Medical Advice." He turned to look sternly at Frank then at her. "I wish you'd reconsider, Mr. Hughes."

"I appreciate your advice, Doctor, but get the form, please."

"I'll see to the rest of the paperwork so you can get home," Mike said. He threw Allison a worried look before following the neurologist out of the cubicle.

Walt lounged against the wall, arms crossed, staring at her. "I assume you know who this is, Allison? If anything happens with someone of his position, I'd hate to think what the repercussions might be." He studied her. "I had no idea you were friends with—"

"She doesn't need you telling her about her friends, Doctor. And I'd appreciate your restraint when it comes to the rest of the staff. No one needs to know what I do since it has no bearing on why I'm here."

"Huh!" Walt pushed himself away from the wall. "Call if you need help tonight, Allison. And I hope you make sure he pays for the fence, *and* your hospitality," he advised before leaving.

"What is it with you people and fences?" Frank allowed her to help him with his socks and pants. He slid off the bed to stand beside her while he finished. She put his shoes at his feet and tied them to keep him from bending. "Can we go now? I really do have a bitch of a headache."

"I'm sure you do. I'm beginning to feel one myself." She untied the back of the gown and handed him his shirt.

He dug a cell phone out of his pants and handed it to her. "Press three and hold it. My doctor said he wants to talk to you if I'm fool enough to leave and you're fool enough to take me home."

Would the night never end? While Frank buttoned his shirt, Allison introduced herself to his doctor and answered a barrage of questions about her experience, where she lived in relation to the hospital and how she would handle Frank's care during the night. Finally, he seemed satisfied, if not pleased, and she disconnected.

She took Frank's arm to lead him to the nurses' station, but he didn't budge.

"I'm sorry if I assumed too much tonight. About staying at your house, I mean." He spoke in a low voice. "I didn't want to stay here. That probably seems strange to you."

166

"Yes, it does." she said just as softly, "Although I think I understand at least some of what's bothering you, staying here would have been so much better for you."

"I'm not risk-averse but I assure you, I'm not a reckless man. I've thought through my options." He cleared his throat and dropped his voice yet again. "I'm in an unusual situation. I find that I'm somewhat in need right now. You strike me as a person I can rely on, and that's no small matter for someone like me. I'll manage whatever I need to, but I'd feel better being somewhere private while I feel my way through this problem." There was no humor in his short laugh. "No pun intended."

"Who *are* you? I mean I know your name because I read your chart, but I must have missed something."

"Can I tell you on the way home? I have a real bitch—"

She sniffed. "I know, I heard." Taking his elbow with one hand and jacket with the other, she guided him to the desk.

They completed the paperwork remarkably fast and were out of the ER in only a few minutes. Neither spoke as they buckled themselves in the car, then Frank leaned his head against the seat, adjusting so the sore section in back was relieved of further pressure. He heaved a sigh.

She let him rest, using the time to process everything that had happened since leaving the reunion. Her tree and fence were damaged, as was the man who'd caused the damage. His blindness was horrible, and she said a swift prayer he would recover quickly.

With instincts developed during years of caring for people, Allison knew a few things about Frank. His fear and almost visceral disgust with feeling helpless broke her heart. Despite the grumpiness he'd shown and his need to command, he was a good man. His eyes, hazel with little gold flecks, topped by bushy brows, were intense. There would be no hiding or turning from his look if he held you in the power of his stare. She imagined the trepidation one could experience under the steady gaze of those eyes.

Or the approval.

Or the kindness.

Or the desire. The thought made her shiver.

There was something about him, even without the strength she knew his piercing gaze would add. He couldn't see her, yet she'd already known the kind of magic he could wield, when she'd touched his face before going to the hospital. The way he'd leaned into her hand had shaken her to the core. She'd wanted to kiss him, to hold him close and more.

As though they'd been friends instead of strangers, she'd understood that giving himself over to someone else's care was alien to his nature. But she'd wanted Frank to give himself over to her. And she'd wanted to put herself into *his* care, knowing somehow the action would be right and good.

Which was why she hadn't fought his coming home with her with more zeal. He needed her, at least until someone came for him tomorrow and took him home. And she needed him, to get past the fiasco of the evening and the feeling of loneliness that had plagued her ever since learning of the reunion. Having someone close by tonight would be a help, for both of them.

She slowed after turning onto the narrow county road a few miles from her house. "Are you watching for deer?" he asked.

"I thought you were sleeping. Yes, I always watch for deer, but sometimes being alert doesn't make a difference. They're experts at jumping out in front of you."

He snorted. "Tell me about it."

"I'm sorry you got hurt, but I'm glad you didn't hit the deer. That would have been bad for the animal, of course, and maybe a lot worse for you, considering how small your car is." She slowed again, for a curve. "Now, obviously the ER staff knows something about you that I don't. What is it? Are you famous?"

His chuckle was low and soft, spreading warmth through her. If he could do that with a laugh, what could he do if they were together, naked in her—

"I can't be too famous if you don't know who I am, can I?"

She shook herself mentally, forcing her voice to sound normal. As though she hadn't just imagined his face hovering inches away, his lips descending to hers.

"Well, yes actually, you could. I'm not exactly what you'd call widely traveled." She'd managed to get through two sentences with only a slight hint of strain. She dug deep for the sense of professionalism she would need to get through the night.

"I see." He seemed to consider that fact before continuing. "I'm not famous. I'm simply the owner of a company. To know who I am you'd have to pay pretty close attention to the stock market. Believe me, I'm really not anyone you should've heard of."

"Is your company big?"

"Pretty big, yes. Now tell me why you're not widely traveled."

"My parents were older when they had me. By the time I went to college my mom was sick. I went to school close by so I could help Dad with her. After Mom died, I couldn't leave him alone with the house and farm. When *he* got sick, I stayed to care for him until he died, year before last."

"I'm sorry," he murmured.

Allison was quiet, remembering those years. There'd been so many of them filled with illness. But filled with laughter, too. She couldn't regret a moment of her time at home, not when she'd been able to help the two most important people in her life.

"Thanks. It's okay. Anyway, after that I got caught up in lots of different things and there never seemed to be a good time to steal away. I will someday, maybe."

"There's no husband or boyfriend to whisk you away?"

Chuckling, she turned into the driveway and the headlights swept the front pasture for the second time that night. "No, there's no one waiting patiently to sweep me off to exotic places." She slowed on the gravel of the driveway. "Your car's still here," she announced.

"Someone will come tomorrow to get the car and fix the fence." He sounded preoccupied.

"Tomorrow's Sunday."

Now he was firm, his voice confident. "Someone will be here tomorrow, trust me."

Shaking her head in disbelief, she pulled away. When she stopped at the foot of the steps leading to the front porch, Frank climbed out before she could make her way to his door. Standing at the front of the Jeep, she spent a moment to observe him.

He leaned against the car, showing the day's weariness. His shoulders slumped. Head bowed, his eyes were shut, those long, glorious lashes resting on his cheek. His mouth turned down at the edges in tiredness rather than upset. But when she rustled up beside him, he raised his head and straightened his shoulders.

Proud man. "I can't imagine why I bought this dress," she said with a sigh at the noise she made. "I can't wait to get out of it."

A slow smile transformed Frank's face from weariness to interest. "I could help with that, you know." Unerringly he placed his arm across her shoulders and drew her to him. "You're cold," he said, wrapping both arms around her.

"I forgot my shawl in the car. This is a sundress, and more suitable to summer than spring." Extricating herself, she took his arm and led the way to the steps. "That is, if the rag is suitable to *any* season," she muttered. "Okay, Frank, there are ten steps. Here's the railing. Just take your time."

He took the first few, slowly but surely. "I *like* that dress."

"You're doing fine, take it easy." She had a firm grasp on his free arm lest he trip on a riser. "Well, as Mike pointed out earlier, you can't see."

"But I will," he vowed with a low growl, "and the next time I offer to help you out of the damn thing, I'll make sure you want it, too."

Dee S. Knight

Chapter Three

Why in hell did I say that? He had no intention of staying around long enough to get to know this woman, clothed or not. In fact, his had been a purely lustful remark, instigated by her comment. For now, he'd just as soon she stay in the dress, regardless of what it looked like. The noise let him know she was near, and somehow that was more comforting than anything else he could think of at the moment. When the thought of simply having a woman nearby was better than the idea of having sex with her, things had gotten to a pretty grim point.

From the minute he'd discovered his blindness, panic had interlaced with cold anger. Anger that he couldn't control fate, and in the current situation couldn't command what he did, or where or with whom. Panic because he didn't know how long his disability—he had to swallow hard even to think the term—would last.

For a man who had risen on his own terms to a powerful position in one of the country's largest electronics firms, helplessness was an intolerable situation.

Currently, he was fighting a raging battle with a competitor, Stanley Maxwell, for a huge government contract. If word of his accident and the resulting blindness got out, he'd be at a serious disadvantage. He'd used the power of his name, his leadership, his vision—a laughable concept, considering his predicament now—to put NicHughes Electronics at the top of the bids for the project. If he had to fight a lengthy health problem while marketing himself as whole and focused on the new NASA job, he had no doubt Maxwell Industries would be able to cut him off at the knees. And Stanley Maxwell would do it, too.

But when Allison was nearby, both panic and anger receded for a while. He didn't understand why, he simply accepted the fact. That's partly why he'd wanted to come home with her tonight instead of staying in the hospital, and probably why he found himself voicing normal male thoughts around her.

Of course, even though he felt better with her around, the blindness was still with him. She couldn't make *that* go away.

All night he'd walked a thin line. Having to reveal information to the hospital without making a big deal of who he was. Hoping in a town this small no newspaper would think to have a reporter standing by, waiting for some big shot executive to be wheeled in, blinded. He hadn't wanted to say too much to anyone for fear the choice tidbit of having one of America's wealthiest men in their local hospital proved too tempting not to share. The city papers would have reporters down here in nothing flat if word got out. He hoped the one loud-mouthed doctor would keep quiet about his identity, and he counted on David to take care of everything else.

Including the reason he was here to begin with. If it hadn't been for that award he'd agreed to present, he would have gone back to DC using a different route and not run through a fence or struck an oak tree. If Martin Johnson's wife had waited to have her baby, and Martin had been able to present the award, he'd be home right now having a nightcap before bed, instead of feeling his way to the porch of a stranger's house.

The whole night had been a series of coincidences. In addition to NicHughes Electronics, Frank had long ago started a philanthropic foundation to reward people who made real contributions to their communities. His being the founder of Helping Hands wasn't generally known since he purposefully stayed in the background, handling only oversight on major issues. Martin Johnson, the man who was the face of Helping Hands, had been unable to come to Lexington because his wife had gone into delivery three weeks early. Frank had been in West Virginia handling the bid on another project and agreed to go through Lexington to present the award on his way back to Washington.

Just in time, the plaque had been over-nighted to him and he'd stuck the unopened package in his suitcase on the way out of the hotel. He'd run late, then sat in stopped traffic on the interstate a few miles outside town. In a fit of impatience, he'd torn off at an exit, driving back roads to find his way into Lexington. He must have missed a sign in his haste, because darkness started to fall and he was still wandering around the countryside. A deer ventured onto the road, and suddenly he saw a fence, then an oak tree, getting closer by the second. The only good thing to happen in a whole night of horrible coincidences was that he wasn't seriously—well, permanently, he hoped—injured. And Allison, of course. Thank God she'd come home early from her reunion.

Considering the weight of the projects he had on his plate at the moment, that he would be incapacitated doing something so small as presenting a good citizen award was almost laughable.

"Good! You made the porch. Not much farther and you can comfortably rest. For a good portion of the night, anyway." Allison sounded almost as relived as he felt. "You have to step up into the house, then no more stairs tonight."

They crossed the porch. He waited while she opened the door then followed her across the threshold.

The house felt cool and smelled fresh, as though windows were open. Under the freshness he caught the scent of citrus, then furniture polish and finally, from somewhere, a hint of flowers.

"Down here," she said after closing the door and taking his arm again. They walked down a hall. The sound of his shoes on hardwood flooring joined the noise her dress made, but the reverberation was contained as it wouldn't be in an open room. Moving slowly, she finally turned into a room to their right.

"This is my office, but the sofa in here pulls out into a double bed. I'm sure this is not what you're used to, but I hope it will do for the night. At least you won't have to deal with any more steps. There's a half bath under the stairs. Do you want to go there now, while I get the bed ready?"

"Yes, please." She guided him, putting his hands on the toilet tank, then turned him so he could feel the sink.

"Can you find your way back? Across the hall, first door on the right."

"I can find it." He sounded much surer than he felt.

She left, closing the door behind her. Seconds later he could no longer hear her as she disappeared into other parts of the house. For the first time since she'd found him sitting in her pasture, hours ago he was certain, he was alone. Bracing his hands on the countertop, he hung his head and gave in to fatigue and worry. And fear. God, would the fear never go away? The doctors had assured him that his problem was probably the temporary medical condition they'd described, but what if the blindness turned out to be atypical and permanent? *Oh, God! What if, what if...?*

He straightened, forcing such weakening thoughts from his mind. He'd overcome a great deal in getting to his current position, and he'd overcome anything else in order to stay there. Nothing had stopped him, and nothing would.

With less difficulty than he might have imagined, he took care of business then crossed the hall and felt his way to the doorway. He could hear Allison now, moving around and snapping a sheet open to put on the bed.

"Can you wait right there for a minute, or do you need to sit?"

"I'm okay," he said.

"I didn't think about clothing. Maybe I should have strapped your suitcase to *your* back."

He chuckled. "I won't need anything tonight, and David will be here in the morning. He'll take care of everything."

"David is your...?"

The softest sound hit his ears. A pillow being shaken into a case? He'd never noticed before the little background noises of everyday life. Is this what it would be like from now on? Hearing sounds and trying to place them for what they were and where they were? His heart rose to his throat. God, he didn't think he was brave enough to live like this if it turned out....

He forced himself to take a breath. "David Wills. He's my assistant."

"You're lucky to have someone to help out in a time like this." She moved around, making other noises he couldn't identify. "I usually leave my windows open at night. Do you want me to open one in here for you?"

"No, I'm okay."

She came right up to him. He felt her breath tickle the hair where his shirt was unbuttoned at the collar. Her hand was cool on his forehead and cheek, the hand of an exceptional and proud woman, as starched as the material in her dress most of the time. He'd discovered that in her no-nonsense treatment of him. But he sensed the softness she kept below the surface. The desire to relieve others of suffering and the willingness to take their needs onto herself. A cross between caregiver and lover. All of that was conveyed in her touch and the way her voice had sounded when she spoke of tending for her parents. Not widely traveled perhaps, but he knew she'd seen things he never had, in the eyes of patients she'd cared for. Absolute trust, gratitude, perhaps a kind of love. He wondered what she saw in his eyes.

"Has your headache worsened?"

"I hate to think what I'd feel like if it did."

She took his arm and guided him to the edge of the bed. "It's been a horribly long night for you. Sleep is what you need. Sorry I'll have to interrupt it a few times before morning." She stooped and began to unlace his shoes.

He jerked his foot away. "What the hell! I can do that." Christ! He'd sounded harsh, but he didn't want this woman on her knees helping him like he was a cripple, a helpless blind man.

"I know you can. I wanted to help." She didn't sound upset or hurt, but she stopped.

The rush of anger left him. "I'm sorry. I'm not used to this. I can get undressed by myself."

"Goodnight, then. I'll see you in a couple of hours." She stood and left the room. Moments later he heard both the swish of the dress and her footfall as she climbed steps, then movement on the floor above him.

Heaving a deep sigh, he bent to finish the job she'd started on his shoes. Not caring where he left them or his clothes, he felt along to where the bed gave way to sofa and slipped between the sheets. They smelled like sunshine, as though they'd been dried outside on a line instead of in a clothes dryer. The scent brought back memories of his boyhood and before he knew it, headache notwithstanding, he was soundly asleep.

* * * *

"*Fuck!*"

The word carried through the house milliseconds before the sound of shattered glass.

Bolting out of bed and instinctively sliding into the slippers she kept nearby, Allison checked the time, turned off the alarm, and ran downstairs.

179

"Frank!" Her hand slammed the light switch on.

He sat on the side of the bed, elbows on knees, head in his hands.

"Are you all right?" With one sweep of her eyes she took in everything. His shoes lay between the bed and her desk and glass covered the floor around the desk. Her heart twisted when she saw the beautiful Waterford lamp her parents had bought when she was a child, laying in shards and splinters. She moved so she could see his feet. "Frank, are you all right? You didn't cut yourself?" There was no sign of blood anywhere.

"I'm okay. I didn't step in any glass." His voice was muffled since he didn't raise his head. "I tripped over my shoe and knocked something over. I'm sorry."

"It's okay, as long as you aren't hurt."

"What did I hit?"

"Just a lamp, Frank." Carefully, she kept any sound of grief for the broken piece from her voice. It had been on the desk—her father's desk—almost as long as she could remember. "I should have moved it away from the edge."

"So the blind man wouldn't break it?" His words vibrated with bitterness and pain.

"No," she said slowly, sitting on the edge of the bed, "so you wouldn't be hurt in the case of a mishap. It was just bad luck, you know. I could have knocked it over myself, hundreds of times." With one last regretful look at the remains of the lamp, she put steel in her voice. "You were getting up for a reason. If you'll swing to this side of the bed you'll be out of harm's way. I'll get the broom and clean up the mess."

She stood and was almost to the door when he brought her to a halt. "Was the lamp valuable?"

Trying for a smile in her tone she asked, "Does it make a difference?"

"The sound was of something solid and long-lasting hitting the floor, yet you've made a bigger deal out of the fence than the lamp." He raised his head, waiting for her answer, as though what she said mattered.

"I admit I'm sad. The lamp was old and had lots of value to me. I can't replace it like I can fix the fence. But I know you, Frank, and I know you're not careless or malicious. Accidents happen. Please don't make the situation more than that."

Allison didn't wait to see his reaction, and when she came back with the broom and vacuum cleaner he was in the bathroom. It didn't take long to brush up the larger pieces of glass. When she'd finished vacuuming the area thoroughly to be sure she had every particle off the floor, she turned to see him in the doorway. He was naked from the waist up. His slacks were zipped, but unbuttoned.

"I think it's safe to come in now."

He didn't move. Though she knew he couldn't see her, and she no longer had on the rustling taffeta dress, his eyes followed her as she pushed the vacuum far out of the traffic path, and set the broom and dustbin aside.

"What time is it?" His stance was casual enough, one arm resting on the doorjamb. But she could feel the tension in him from across the room.

"Almost two. I would have been coming down to wake you in a few minutes." Four strides took her to the bed, where she straightened the covers and fluffed the pillows.

Suddenly, the light went out. Thin moonlight barely illuminated the room, but she could see Frank move unerringly toward her. Maybe he *could* see.

Before she formulated the right questions, he enveloped her in his arms and rested his cheek on her head. "I wanted us to be on equal footing for a minute, while I tell you something."

Her heart raced, feeling his heat against her. *This is wrong*, a part of her brain screamed. *This man is a patient.*

But she'd known almost from the first that he was no ordinary patient. Certainly no ordinary man. His appearance in her life had been like magic, at the very moment she'd felt most alone.

Placing her hands on his waist, she neither embraced him nor pushed away. She just absorbed the feel of him.

"I'm sorry, Allison."

"For what?"

"For the fence, the lamp, for all the trouble. For being shitty when you were doing everything in your power to help me. I'm sorry for all of it. I just hope you understand."

"I think I do," she whispered. She did then what she'd wanted to do almost since meeting him. Her arms slid around his waist. His heartbeat, steady under her ear, sped up as he lightly pressed her head against him, holding her where she could sense the very core of him. A shudder passed through him; she felt as though it had run through her.

"I'm afraid." Now the drumbeat of his heart was so loud, it filled her head.

For a man like Frank, fear must have been the hardest thing in the world to admit.

She nodded against his chest. "I know what you're thinking. What if the doctors are wrong."

The breath he released was like a live thing between them, felt as well as heard.

"Yes. *What ifs* have been plaguing me all night. I'm scared shitless, Allison, and I don't know what to do. All my life there've been alternatives. Not always good ones, but some action I could take to affect an outcome. I'm at a loss here. Powerless."

"Frank, the crash just happened. You have to give yourself time to heal."

"You don't know what it's like, being handicapped when so much rides on your being in charge. Not you! Not with your magic touch, you wouldn't know how I feel." He groaned into her hair.

His pain washed over her, and she tightened her arms. He responded, crushing her to him.

"What can I do to help you?"

"Lend me some of your strength. Tell me I'm going to be all right. Say it over and over until I believe you. Don't leave me alone in the dark, with nothing but my thoughts for company." His breath hitched. "Please."

She leaned back to look into his face. Tears glistened in his eyes and he turned away. With a finger to his chin she brought his head back. Cupping his neck below his ear, she stroked her thumb across his cheek.

"Shall I tell you a secret now? I need you tonight, too. I need your warmth and comfort. Please hold me. Make me feel like a woman, not a nurse or just another volunteer. Not someone everyone knows will be available on Saturday night to fill in an extra shift. But someone desired."

He relaxed his hold ever so slightly, some of the stiffness leaving him.

"Stress won't help you heal faster," she said, "so let go of that drive for perfection. Until you're healed, just think about yourself."

Physician, heal thyself, she thought. Maybe her life would have different if she'd given more thought to herself as she healed. *Had* she ever healed, truly? From the accident all those years ago, and then from her parents' illnesses and deaths?

Speaking to herself as well as Frank, she added, "Give yourself permission to be selfish and just think about what's best for you."

"And you," he amended.

Smiling, she leaned against him again. "Okay, you can take on the burden of me. I'll gladly take the gift of your holding me tonight, and when you leave tomorrow I hope we'll both be better off."

By unspoken consent, they got into bed, breaking apart to move to opposite sides then coming together again like iron to a magnet. He wore his briefs, she her nightgown. Neither sought sex, just the other's touch.

Quietly, held in his arms, Allison spoke of growing up on the farm. She described her parents and her uncle John, who lived on the next farm with his two sons and helped with her sheep. She portrayed in vivid words the seasons of her life in the Virginia mountains. The thrill of walking through the woods while being showered with dogwood petals, summer picnics held on slabs of rock in the middle of rushing streams, crisp air and golden leaves, and winters of sledding down the hill into the back pasture. She didn't mention falling from her horse, crawling up the hillside of brambles or pushing herself in a painful effort to get home, thus making the injuries much worse than they would have been. Left out was the psychological pain the scars and limp caused, which affected her activities and view of the world. No, she'd kept the accident that had changed her life forever to herself.

Frank told of growing up in a row of dark tenement houses in Chicago, where the winters were cold but the wind whipping from the lake made them twice as frigid. Describing his friends, he managed to make her laugh at their pranks, which he hinted were just inside the boundary of the law. There was no happy talk of family outings or afternoons spent with his parents and brother.

But his voice took on a sense of wonder when he explained his love affair with math and science, and how a casual interest finally turned to dedication. A note of pride crept into his tone when he told how his discipline and focus had earned him a scholarship to the university—the first person in his family to attend.

"Your parents must have been beside themselves with pride when you graduated," she said.

He shrugged. "I guess my mother was happy, I don't know. My dad died right after high school graduation and mom remarried soon afterward. We talk every few weeks, but I don't see her or my brother much. Truthfully, I don't think I ever looked back after I left there, so I'm not sure I would have known if they were proud of me."

He shifted closer to her. "I admire that you took such good care of your folks. Especially your mother, when you could have been off at school, enjoying yourself. They needed you and you were here for them. I think at that age I might have been too selfish to do the right thing."

"I doubt you have a selfish bone in your body."

He snorted. "Sorry to disappoint you, but you don't get where I am in business without being selfish."

She raised on her elbow and looked at him, seeing the outline of his features in the pale light. Her nipples pressed through the thin material of her nightgown and rubbed his side. Mentally she caught her breath at the sensuousness of their contact. The hitch she heard in his breath was literal. "I'm a very good judge of character."

"You must be some kind of judge, or you'd be pretty nervous pressing against me like that. You feel so damn good, Allison. In my mind I want you more than I've ever wanted a woman. Unfortunately, I don't think I can do anything about it. God knows, I wish I could."

"No stress, remember? What we've just shared has been wonderful." She touched his forehead. "Your head still hurts."

He nodded. "How did you know?"

"Magic." With a few presses on the small buttons, she set her watch alarm to go off in two hours. Then she pulled herself up and kissed him

186

with all the tenderness she could muster. "Come here." He turned to her and she wrapped her arm around him, softly stroking his head with her free hand. "Try to sleep. I've got you."

Nestling his head against her breasts he murmured, "I can hear your heart, Allison. Can you hear mine?" With a soft sigh, he draped his arm over her hip and fell asleep.

* * * *

Half asleep, he'd first thought he was having a wet dream. His mouth was very near a nipple and with only a slight movement, he captured the nub, sucking it through some flimsy material. The action was all the more erotic through the now-wet fabric. His tongue swirled over it, teasing, savoring, and finally causing the woman he was with to moan in pleasure.

Yeah, baby. With her moan, his cock became hard as steel. He rubbed the hard ridge along her thigh.

Never. He'd never been so aroused. Well, maybe the first time or two he'd had a woman, but that was as a boy, when all he could think about was getting off. In all the years since, as he'd come to appreciate the chase, the seduction and the conquest, there had never been a moment like he felt now. Before, the satisfaction had come from the process of winning. Now, in his dream, there was nothing more than the sheer heat of the woman he held and the thrill of knowing she wanted him as much as he wanted her.

When she used a gentle touch on his nape to hold him closer, he realized he was awake. Where he was and who he was with hit him like a blow. It was Allison's nipple his tongue teased, Allison's thigh he rubbed, Allison's body he wanted to be inside or die. This wasn't some broad, or even a casual friend he'd brought home for an evening of mutually satisfying sex. This was no quick fuck, this was *Allison*.

She wanted him, of that he was certain. Last night she let him know when she'd said she needed to be held and desired as a woman. He didn't think Allison was the kind of woman who said that to just any man, so she must have felt the same spark between them he did.

His mind grasped the point, even as his body moved past caring.

Was she even awake? He wasn't sure. Her body moved against his, and soft whimpers escaped her lips. His hand moved down her thigh, finally reaching the hem of her gown. Sliding his hand under, he smoothed the thin material back up her leg, kneading her soft ass when he reached it.

With no effort at all, he pushed her to her back, bringing his hand from the cheeks of her butt to the soft curls of her pussy. She released his neck and squirmed, sighing and stretching. Her arms didn't settle at her side, so they must be raised. Such trust—she'd left her body wide open to him.

"Allison? Are you awake?" His voice was no softer than his touch, as his fingers combed through her curls, inching to that secret place he knew she wanted him to be.

"Hmm-hmm. How's your head?"

He chuckled for the first time in what felt like forever. "Oh, my head feels a lot better." Dipping the head in question to lick her nipple, he pressed his hand against her mound. She parted her legs, allowing him the access he craved. He stroked her clit, gently at first then more insistently before searing a path down her stomach with his tongue.

"Frank?" She breathed his name.

"Hmm?" He buried his face in her pussy. The scent of her arousal forced even more blood rushing to his groin. He didn't know how he could stand much more. She smelled sweet, so sweet, and he wanted her. God, yes! All of her. With a lightning caress, his tongue swept across her clit, while one finger worked in and out of her slick, hot lips.

"Frank!"

Sneaking another, longer lick, confirmed his first thought. She tasted even better than she smelled.

He raised his head, forgetting for a moment that he couldn't see. *There* was a joke he wouldn't be able to tell anyone. *"Guess what I can do as well without sight as with?"*

The motion of his finger never ceased, even as he answered her.

"What is it, sweetheart?" For her, he wanted to sound in command and sophisticated. But even to his own ears, his voice, low and raspy, gave him away as being like any other man who was dying to screw a woman. The common touch wasn't good enough for Allison.

"What you're doing feels so good, but please...please...please, Frank."

She hadn't finished her plea before he was standing, ripping his briefs off. "Take off your nightgown. I can't see you, but I want to feel all of you against all of me."

The sofa bed squeaked and he heard her softly grunt. *Taking off her gown.* Several squeaks. *Allison lying back, moving to the center.*

"I'm ready."

Her voice, half hoarse with desire, half shy, filled him with awe that she could feel both with him. *For* him. Two words. Yet they meant so much. In his heart, he knew a promise that making love with Allison would be something momentous, earth-shattering. Something that could change his life.

Now was not the time to analyze what was about to happen, however. He pushed it from his mind, needing to keep what they were doing simple, wanting nothing more than to bring each of them pleasure.

He knelt on the bed, gingerly reaching for her. She took his hand and covered her breast. Breathing became difficult. What was wrong with him? It's not like she was his first. In fact, he didn't want to think how many there had been before her.

"Before" didn't matter now. Allison was special.

He scooted to her, immediately stretching out between her parted legs. Braced on one elbow, he used his other hand to glide the head of his penis between her lips.

"Oh, my God," she groaned.

"I can't wait too long," he gasped in reply.

"Don't! Please don't."

"I won't. I won't, baby." With one smooth thrust he entered her.

Her legs bent and came up around his waist. Raising his hips caused the most fantastic sensation. He wouldn't hold out long at this rate. She was so *tight*, like she hadn't been with a man in a long while. The thought made him absurdly happy.

"You're tight, sweetheart, and so hot. I love being in you."

Her hands were all over his shoulders and arms, stroking his skin as he stroked her clit with his cock. Her legs spread even wider.

"When you're inside me it's as though this is the way life should be." Her hips rose to meet him. "Oh!"

Her nipples brushed his chest as they moved. He increased the sweet friction by leaning forward to take her lips. She opened for him and he thrust his tongue into her in rhythm with his hips. Wrapping her arms around him, she pulled him onto her.

"Too heavy," he whispered.

"I want it, please. Faster."

"Yes."

She sucked his tongue as he gave her his cock, hard and fast. Within seconds she screamed into his mouth.

Holy shit! Her contractions were so powerful, cascading along the length of him. He held fast, reveling in pure sensation. When she calmed somewhat, he withdrew and thrust hard, setting her off again.

Pulling his mouth away he pushed up and off her, driving once more, so deeply he thought he touched the back of her womb. Whether reality or imagination, that image was enough to make him erupt.

The emotion was too sweet. Too sweet to cry out, to yell, to call her name. He couldn't put the world into rational perspective, couldn't think of what came next, couldn't imagine what life would be if he couldn't have her again and again.

With one last push, he emptied himself, all the while feeling the swell of her climax crash around him, over him, strengthening his release. His lungs were like bellows and his heart raced.

Easing himself down to her, he took her lips tenderly even as he tried to steady his breathing. She framed his face with her hands and brushed her tongue across his lips. He rained soft, quick kisses on her cheeks and eyelids before resting his forehead on hers.

"Has it been a long time for you?" He was still inside her, not hard like he had been but with the heart-stopping certainty he could go again with little stimulation. This from sex with a woman he hadn't even known for twenty-four hours? There had to be more to what they shared than mere attraction.

She wrapped her legs around his, saying without words that she didn't want him to move. "Since I've been with someone? Yes, a long time. Since being with a man has felt like *this*? It's never been like this."

That was all he needed. With a low groan he stiffened, rocking his hips to let her know. His contact was a nudge, asking permission to love her again. Her knees caressed his waist, her heels brushed his butt. She was ready, and he had provided plenty of lubrication. It crossed his mind then, that she was filled already with *him*, his semen, and he found the idea to be the most erotic he'd ever had.

He moved in her again, slowly, setting a rhythm designed for pleasure, not relief. In concert, her hips met his, rolling, grinding, enticing him to speed. With effort, he resisted.

The notion that he could perform as well without his sight wasn't quite right. In so many ways it was better. He'd never considered before how important sound was in sex. Having a light on to watch the effects of his actions on the face of his lover was arousing. But he didn't think he'd ever paid as much attention to soft moans, whimpers from the back of the throat, the slick sound of his cock moving in and out of a wet pussy, the puffs of exhaled air with each stroke. Even the squeak of bed springs in union with his thrusts increased his need.

And the smell. Lord! Simply inhaling deeply and scenting Allison was enough to drive him crazy. He pictured them as they were at that moment, their arousal hanging in the room like an erotic incense.

He'd always appreciated touch, and her skin was smooth and soft. But forever after he'd remember Allison's taste. In the past, licking a woman's neck had titillated them both—her skin against the semi-roughness of his tongue. But when he licked Allison's neck, or her nipple, as he was now, the salty tang he tasted came from her exertions loving him, and added a whole new dimension to his senses. The taste of her cream was unique and he knew he would always live with the memory.

He paced himself. As great as this felt, he knew it couldn't equal the intensity of the last climax. So he concentrated on long, sure strokes, designed to bring her maximum pleasure. Moans resonating from deep inside her meant he was succeeding.

"Ohgodohgodohgod!" She arched off the bed, gripping his arms, gasping for breath.

Impossible as it was to believe, her contractions were as strong as they had been before. He'd expected ripples. Instead he felt her strong muscles grasp, release, grasp, release. He wished he could pause and experience the thrill, but the very stimulation he wanted to enjoy pushed him over the edge. Before he was aware, he shot into her again, throbbing against her tight sheath.

His climax either lasted forever or was over in seconds. He didn't know or care. Time had no meaning.

He laid his head beside hers and tried to catch his breath. Her hands rested on his waist, her legs fell to the bed beside his. This time, his penis slid from her, limp.

Finally, she broke the silence. "I guess I should clean up."

He moved to the side, and she scrambled from the bed. Too late, he thought, feeling the wet spot in the center of the mattress. He bolted upright. *Too late!* He hadn't used a condom and hadn't thought to ask her about birth control. Hadn't thought to ask her about *anything*. The idea of his semen filling her was a great turn-on, but he'd given no thought to consequences.

"You're a dumb shit, Hughes," he muttered. He raked his hand through his hair, wincing and jerking his hand away when he hit the tender spot at the back of his head. "A blind, stupid, dumb shit who was only thinking of himself."

Unable to lie still and wait for her to return, Frank edged out of bed and groped his way to the hall. There he paced. A short distance up, a short distance back, keeping a finger in contact with the wall. He heard the toilet flush, water run in the sink, a drawer open and close. Finally, the door opened.

"Oh, I'm sorry. I shouldn't have taken so long."

"No, I need to ask you. Are you on birth control?"

She hesitated.

"Because we didn't use anything." He brushed his hand across his head again, taking care not to come near the sore area. Pacing again, he continued worriedly, "I can't remember the last time I had sex without some form of protection. God damn it, I don't know when I've been so careless."

He didn't hear her move beside him. "It's okay, Frank. I'm a nurse, remember? I know about such things. There's nothing at all for you to worry about."

"No?" The reprieve from responsibility was overwhelming. For once, he wasn't the person having to worry. Someone else was in control and everything was all right. He could rely on Allison, as he had for almost everything else these past several hours.

"Put it right out of your mind." She took his arm and they slowly made their way into the office. "Now, did we make too big a mess? Do I need to get fresh sheets?"

She released him and began to move away. Before she could escape he reached out and pulled her into his arms. "Yeah, there's a mess, but think of how we made the mess." Holding her close he nuzzled her ear. "I've never known anyone like you, Allison. Not being able to see heightened all my other senses. Your scent, your touch. Every whimper and sigh pushed me on. Your taste! My God, your taste. If you hadn't already worn me out, I'd get hard again just remembering the flavor of Allison on my tongue."

She said nothing, but he felt her softness mold to him. Her hands linked behind his back, her mouth, pressed against his chest, turned up in a smile. He cupped her butt and pulled her tighter, his penis becoming semi-erect even after their recent activity.

"I've never told any woman all I told you tonight. I've never slept with a woman without sex like we did earlier. My senses have never been stretched to fever pitch like they were a little while ago. Twice. I want to say thank you."

"Oh." Turning her head so her ear was over his heart, she was quiet for a moment. "I guess I don't know what to say to that, this situation being new to me, too. I enjoyed our talk. I loved holding you and being held. The sex was...well, incredible. I needed you, Frank, and you gave me more than I could have hoped for. No thanks are needed."

He gave her a light squeeze.

"But sleeping with you was wrong of me. You're my patient, not my lover."

Guilt in her voice tugged at his heart. He didn't want regret to pull at the edges of the wonder and joy he'd hoped to instill in her. Certainly he didn't want anything to dispel the sense of contentment he felt being with her.

"Not tonight." Skimming his hand across her hair, he appreciated the soft, silky texture threading through his fingers. "That wet spot is you and me. Think you can handle it?"

She nodded. "Let's go back to bed." Her whisper in the night was all he needed or wanted.

* * * *

After assuring her that he felt much better, they went to sleep, spoon fashion. Her watch alarm went off a couple of hours later and she woke him, although she was pretty certain from his earlier activity that he was all right.

Once awake, he didn't seem to want to let go of the moment. He kissed her, caressed her, cuddled her against him, all the while whispering the most astonishing sentiments.

"Do you even know how beautiful you are? I'll bet men have told you your whole life."

"I'm not beautiful," she murmured. "If you could take a good look at me, you'd see I'm a plain Jane." She ran her hands across the expanse of his chest, playing with the soft curls that covered it.

He turned to her and she was surprised at how they fit, as though they'd been molded for each other. Lazily, he caressed her breast and thumbed her nipple, and moisture pooled between her legs.

"I don't believe that. I know right now I don't have sight, but I can see you, Allison Hayes, and you're beautiful." He scooted down to suckle her. "And you feel and taste so good, I don't ever want to give this up."

As he sucked, his hand dropped around and below her hips to knead her buttocks. A slow heat built in her. Running her fingers across his nape she emboldened him. He hummed approval, the sound vibrating through her, meeting the heat starting to spiral from her inner core.

When he slipped beneath the covers to eat her, she shivered. There was no denying the fact that the simple acts of placing tongue to clit and lips to nether lips could make one soar to the stars. She was living proof.

With a gentle nudge, he pushed her legs open. They parted further on their own, to provide room for his broad shoulders as his mouth and tongue further explored her.

In a world gone mad with desire, she barely heard his words of encouragement and excitement. At last he quit speaking and all she knew was the feel of his wet mouth suckling her, the quick flick of his tongue stroking her clit and the incessant ebb and flow of his fingers in her slick passage. Then it was she who filled the night with words and sounds. She who cried his name and called for him never to stop.

His breath was hot upon her, the unceasing sweep of his tongue carrying her beyond rational thought. She arched off the bed. With his free hand he reached under her buttocks to press her closer to his hungry mouth and she gladly welcomed the move.

Quicker than she could think, he exchanged fingers for mouth, pressing his thumb firmly on her clit while his tongue felt her release. Holding a deep breath, her body trembled as Frank's silky hair brushed her inner thighs. His breath fanned the flames of the fire his tongue and fingers had started, until finally there was nothing left of her to give.

Gasping, she collapsed. Frank kissed her thighs, nuzzled his head against her mound, then kissed his way up her body. Even her sensitive nipples welcomed the swirl of his tongue. When he reached her mouth, kissing became sinfully decadent as she sampled her musky taste from his lips.

"You taste like sweet honey," he murmured. His hands raked her, touching every part of her he could reach. His erection pressed hard into her stomach.

"What do you taste like, I wonder?"

He shook his head. "Don't feel like you have to if it makes you uncomfortable."

"I want to," she whispered.

Deftly, he turned them so she lay on top. The rhythm of his breathing changed ever so slightly, and his fingers, brushing her hair behind her ears, were full of tension.

"Then I'd like you to," he said in as low a voice, "very much."

She'd taken a man in her mouth before, but reluctantly and not to completion. With Frank, there was no hesitation. When she kissed a path from his ear down his neck, then took time to suckle his nipple, he groaned and begged her not to wait.

Smiling at the power she held over him, she nonetheless gave in to his wish. The truth was, she didn't want to wait, either.

Her fingers slid over the smooth head of his penis and down the thick shaft, skimming veins and the rough texture of his skin until reaching the springy coarse hair at the base. He was so big! Not only thick but long. She wasn't even sure she could fit all of him in her mouth.

Swirling her tongue over the head, and with Frank's moan of pleasure ringing in her ears, she gained courage to take him, a little at a time.

He held steady. She didn't think she even heard him breathe until she had half of him in her mouth. Then he gasped.

His hands grasped her head, his fingers wound through her hair. Slowly he pushed into her, crooning faintly how sweet she was, how wonderful her mouth felt around him, how well she was doing, taking him.

Finally, she had all of him, and she raised up, dragging her tongue along his length. On the descent, she didn't know if he'd stopped talking or if she was concentrating so hard she wasn't listening.

Taking him was easier after she knew what to expect, and she found her timing. When she heard his raspy breath and felt he was close, she made up her mind not to let go of him. She resisted the gentle tug of his hands on her head, pressing down to take all of him as he cried out.

Knowing a sense of fulfillment she never thought possible, she held him tightly as he filled her mouth, and she swallowed his very essence. Her heart pounded, much as when he'd made her come, and she couldn't stop stroking him, with her hands and her tongue.

His breath was still erratic when she settled in his arms. "Let me kiss you," he groaned. He pushed his tongue deep into her mouth in a primal branding, claiming her in a way no one ever had.

Later, after they calmed each other, stroking and caressing, and delivering light kisses, they talked again. Frank explained his concerns about his blindness becoming known. He told her generalities about his job bid and what he feared would happen if word got out about his accident. He gave no details about his firm or who he was, but she didn't mind. Somehow, it didn't seem important. With her he was Frank, not a wealthy man of some celebrity.

"But your blindness is probably temporary," she protested. "How can they hold something against you that won't last?"

"We don't know if it is temporary—at least that's the way the business world will see the situation. I've always been a perfectionist. If something isn't perfect, or especially if I can't make it so, I don't deal with it. My reputation will come back to bite me now if word gets out. I'm very hands-on, so whatever affects me affects the whole company. What I've demanded of others, they'll now demand of me, and if I'm not whole, no one will believe I'll manage the project properly."

"I see," she agreed, sweeping her hand back and forth across his hip, needing to touch him in the time they had left.

Talking and touching. Sex was intimate, but any more intimate than the closeness that came from sharing bits of themselves in the night? She didn't think so.

"I'm sleepy. How about you?" she finally whispered.

"Yes."

In the darkness, she felt rather than saw his smile.

"Are you going to wake me again in another couple of hours? The way we just woke up was very nice."

She chuckled, and was surprised at the low, sexy sound. "You'd like that wouldn't you?"

"What do you think?" Soft as cotton, his tongue brushed her lips.

"Well, I'm not one to shirk my duty so you can be sure I'll be waking you again." Her tongue traced the outline of his lips and he moaned.

"Right. Best not to take any chances," he teased.

"But now, sleep is what you want, sir." Rolling away from him, she was delighted when he reached across her waist and pulled her back against him.

"Not what I want, but what I need," he admitted. His voice was heavy and within moments she heard the steady, deep breathing that signified slumber.

Chapter Four

As the coffee pot gurgled and she finished lightly frying the Canadian bacon, Allison thought about the man on the sofa bed in her office. That wonderful man and how he'd made her feel. Last night had been the most fantastic of her life. True, the evening hadn't started auspiciously, between the horrid dress and everyone's reaction to it, then finding a man crashed in her pasture. But knowing Frank Hughes made everything else worthwhile.

It had been almost four-thirty when they'd stopped talking, and was only ten-thirty now. She'd slipped out of bed a little before eight, careful not to wake him. Now, lifting the coffee pot to pour the first cup of the morning, she wondered how long she should let him sleep.

A knock at the front door took the decision out of her hands. Putting the cup on the table, she hurried so whoever it was wouldn't knock again and wake Frank. Two men stood on the porch.

"Ms. Hayes?" The taller and younger of the pair spoke. He gave her a sharp look, making her self-conscious in her simple slacks and sweater. She put a hand to her hair, glad she'd at least pulled it back in a loose braid instead of leaving it free.

"Yes."

"We're looking for Nic."

She frowned.

He frowned back. "I'm sorry. Nic Hughes. That's his car out there," he added, pointing generally toward the road.

"Oh! Frank. Yes, he's here. Come in, please."

The men entered, the older one with a medical bag. "I'm David Wills. This is Dr. Mark Bowman." David stared candidly at his surroundings. His casual look belied what she imagined he was really doing: taking in everything, evaluating what he saw and then storing it in his memory for later recall.

She regarded him the same way. He was tall, blond, very muscular, maybe late twenties. Except for the taste and cut of his clothes, he would have reminded her of a surf bum—no responsibilities or cares other than catching the next big wave—but she held no illusions. To work closely with Frank, he'd have to be very responsible, bright and savvy.

With his graying hair, clear blue eyes and friendly smile, Dr. Bowman looked the quintessential trusted family doctor. Again, she assumed nothing other than he was top in his field. Frank wouldn't waste time on anything else.

With a sinking heart she remembered his words about dealing only with perfection or something he could make perfect. Thank heaven he hadn't seen her, with her plain face and scars. Or watched how she limped. Last night, he'd been attuned to different aspects of her and happiness filled her at the memory of how they'd satisfied each other. If only they'd had more time, but....

"Frank is still asleep." She turned her attention to the doctor. "It's nice to meet you, Doctor, after our talk last night. I have the chart from the ER for you. He made it through the night very well, with no discernable problems." Hoping she wouldn't blush at how well he'd made it through the night, she forced her most professional attitude forward.

"Wonderful. Thanks."

"Would you like to wash up? There's a bath down the hall on the left. I was just getting things ready for breakfast, so coffee's made if you want some." Pointing down the hall and flicking her finger left, she looked to see that David understood how to reach the kitchen. "I'll get Frank up."

The doctor headed for the bathroom. David turned toward the back of the house and the aroma of brewed coffee, but not until giving her an appraising look.

She took a deep breath, disappointed their magical hours were over. Frank would go back to Washington with David and Dr. Bowman, and she'd never see him again. Was that ache the sign of a broken heart? Impossible after less than one day. "Not even magic works that fast," she murmured.

Tucking away the lover persona and putting on her nurse mask, she stopped outside the office door, knocked, then entered, closing the door behind her. Frank lay on his back, the sheet barely covering his groin. Slightly below that, she saw the outline of his cock lying over his thigh, evidencing a morning erection. She'd never seen his penis, but she knew how it felt and how it tasted. Her panties dampened with the memory, and she wanted more than anything to climb back beside him and take comfort in his arms before they faced the reality of his leaving.

One arm was slung out, where she would have been had she stayed in bed. The other was crooked over his head. He snored lightly, his face roguish with dark bristles covering chin and jaw. His thick black lashes flicked as he dreamed. More than anything in the world, she hated to wake him and let him go.

"Frank?" No response. "*Frank.* Time to wake up."

"Huh?" It was the slightest murmur. Instead of opening his eyes he rolled onto his side.

She took the few steps needed to reach the bed, and sat on the edge. Shaking his shoulder she said, "Time to wake up. Your friends are here."

Slowly his lids raised, revealing his remarkable hazel eyes. He blinked. Took a breath, stretched. "Allison?"

"Yes. How do you feel?" Gently, she rubbed her hand over his shoulder, to his neck and the back of his head where she used fingertips to lightly massage his scalp.

"Not bad. My head's sore there, but my headache is gone." He captured her hand in his and brought it to his lips. "Why'd you get up? Come back to bed."

"No time to sleep. The day's awastin'."

"Who said anything about sleeping, woman?" His smile was brilliant, his voice husky with desire. She glanced at his groin. The half-erect cock she'd guessed at under the sheet now showed itself to be an impressive length and thickness.

"Oh, you're tempting me, but your friends are here."

He came fully awake. "David? Is Mark Bowman with him?" His erection lost its size and he released her hand as he turned to sit.

"Yes. They just arrived. But go slowly and take your time. After you're dressed, just call out. Dr. Bowman will want to examine you, and he can come in here."

The change in him was immediate. He returned to the businessman she'd first met in her pasture the previous night.

"Right. I can handle things now. I'll go to the bathroom and let you know when I'm ready."

"That's fine." The bathroom door opened and she heard Dr. Bowman move past on his way to the kitchen. She stood and looked around the room. "Okay, I'm going to fold the bed away, but your clothes will be laid out on the sofa. I ran all but your slacks through the laundry this morning, so your underwear is clean. I gave your slacks a good brushing. I didn't feel comfortable getting into the car for your suitcase without your knowledge."

"That's great. Thanks." Feeling the wall with his fingertips, he made his way to the door, where he turned toward her. "I really mean that, Allison. Thank you for everything. For last night especially, and I don't mean the sex."

Suddenly she wished she could cry. She wanted to let the tears fall and never stop. But she didn't.

She walked over and moved him aside to open the door. "We'll be listening for you."

Shoulders back and head high, showing none of the fear he'd admitted to during the night, Nic—the businessman—moved across the hall and felt his way to the bathroom. Her Frank, the man she'd comforted and made passionate love to, was gone.

Pushing emotion aside, as she had so many times in her life, Allison prepared the room and then strode to the kitchen to see about fixing her guests something to eat.

*

After rousing Frank, things progressed remarkably quickly. Dr. Bowman reviewed the chart while they waited for Frank to dress, then joined him in the office. She'd looked forward to asking David a few questions about his employer, but he took a key from his pocket and went out to see if the car could be driven.

Allison got a good look at the little silver Porsche when David parked behind an impressive BMW sedan. With amusement, she noted there was more money parked in her front drive than she made in a year. Except for numerous scratches and a bent fender that David pulled away from the tire, nothing much seemed wrong with the sports car. If not for a bump on the head, Frank would have been able to drive away, perhaps calling later to explain about the fence.

Life was full of ifs. If the deer hadn't chosen that moment to run into the road, Frank wouldn't have crashed through her fence at all. If she hadn't left the reunion early, he might have wandered around and gotten more hurt than he was. If she hadn't worn that hideous dress, she probably would have stayed longer to help Mary.

Her expression softened. If she hadn't bought that particular gown, Frank wouldn't have felt the comfort he had, listening to the sound. The dress suddenly took on a new perspective, and it wasn't a hideous one at all.

Dr. Bowman came out of the office walking slowly, acting as guide to Frank. Their arms touched, though scarcely, and as he walked toward the front door, she had to look hard to recognize that Frank was sightless.

"Do you want something to eat? I've started breakfast."

"Thanks, Ms. Hayes," Dr, Bowman said politely, "but I'd just as soon get Nic back to his own home as soon as possible. I think he'll rest better there, and I can keep an eye on any changes."

"Of course," she murmured.

"David?" Frank stopped when the doctor did.

"Yes, Nic."

"How's the car?"

"I'll get it home. Mark can drive the BMW. You'll be more comfortable riding in the sedan."

Frank simply nodded. "What about the fence? People around here take their fences very seriously." He smiled, an open, generous smile, though not particularly directed at her.

David smiled too, watching his boss intently. "I have one of our crews coming out this afternoon." Turning to Allison, he held out a business card. "The foreman's name is Stuart Samuels. He's supposed to check with you so you can give him any specific instructions. Otherwise, they'll repair the fence line and match their work with whatever's there. If you have any problems or questions, don't hesitate to call. My office and cell number are listed on the card."

"That's fine, thank you." She looked at what he'd handed her. *NicHughes Electronics, David Wills.*

"Wait a minute." Eyes wide, she stared at the man she'd spent the night making love with. "Frank, you're *NicHughes Electronics?*"

The smile faded from Frank's face. All eyes were on him, although he had no way of knowing.

"Franklin Nicholas Hughes. Nic Hughes is my business name. I explained to you about business things. Later, anyway." He cleared his throat. "I mean, I didn't know who you were at first. When we finally talked business, details didn't seem important." Turning slightly, he faced her directly, almost as though he could see where she stood. "Is it important?" his tone asked more than the words.

Now all eyes were on her. She understood completely. Nic Hughes was the job. Frank, the man who'd held her heart and soul last night, Frank was the man. "No. It's not important at all."

He gave an almost imperceptible nod.

Straightening her shoulders, she took a deep breath then took his hand. "Take care of yourself, Frank. I hope everything turns out very well for you."

He squeezed her hand. "Thanks. I couldn't have asked for a better person's fence to run through."

She moved aside. With the railing on one side and the doctor on the other, he made his way down the steps and out of her life.

*

Restless, she moved around the kitchen. The dinner dishes had all been put away, the sink scoured. More coffee had been put on to brew, although she knew she'd had enough already to satisfy her caffeine needs for a week.

She sighed, staring through the back screendoor at the sheep walking the wire fence in the lower pasture. Always looking for a way to get someplace new, someplace different than where they were, they searched for where the grass was greener. But they weren't the brightest animals on earth. Even when he found a hole in the fence, a sheep might not see the opening for what it was. Once passed, the ewe or ram might never find the hole again, and so be stuck forever in one pasture until the farmer and his dog came along. Sheep missed many opportunities for greener grass, new pastures, freedom.

Am I like that? Had she passed by chances, not recognizing them for what they were? Or, more likely, had she conveniently ignored them, taking the easier path? Unlike most of her friends, she'd stayed home, not chancing life or love. Had she used her parents and even her childhood accident as an excuse not to spread her wings? She'd always thought when she was ready, she'd do the things other people talked about, things she'd once thought about with enthusiasm herself. Had she let her chances go by, thinking she'd come back to them later? Like the sheep passing the hole in the fence, perhaps she wouldn't find those opportunities again.

With a cup of fresh coffee, she walked outside. She wished Frank were here. The tulips and jonquils were still in riotous bloom, the early azaleas were starting the showy stage of display, and the dogwood was magnificent, at its peak of snowy white and bright pink. With pleasure, she would have described the scene to him as they walked up the drive, and would have seen the world in a different way while she did so. As it was, as *she* was—alone—her beautiful flower beds and pastureland lost some appeal.

She wished she understood this sudden feeling of discomfort in her own home. The reason couldn't really be Frank. He hadn't even been in her life one day—barely a full twelve hours, including time asleep. Yet they were hours enough to dislodge the contentment of a lifetime.

When she reached the end of the drive, she was surprised to see her uncle's truck parked on the side of the road. He and her cousin, Ned, stood examining the new section of fence. She strolled up to them. "What do you think?"

John turned twinkling brown eyes on her. "Never heard such a ruckus with those air compressor nail guns and paint sprayers. Saw them here when we came home from dinner after church. Must have been twenty men putting your fence back together. What happened, anyways?" He stood tall and lean, wearing a flannel shirt mostly concealed by coveralls her aunt insisted on ironing. Much younger than her father, his hair was still white from advancing age, but his eyes showed none of the years his hair color indicated.

Ned spoke up. "If we hadn't known the sheep were in the lower pasture, Allie, we would have come up and fixed the fence. But we figured the work would wait 'til after church." He stuck his hands in his jeans and gave her a curious look before echoing his father. "What happened?" Stance and expression exactly like his father's, Ned showed the Hayes coloring in his auburn hair and dark brown eyes.

"A man ran through the fence last night. He needed someone to look after him and didn't want to stay at the hospital so I said he could sleep on the sofa in the office." She shrugged. "This is his way of making amends."

Her uncle whistled and cast an appreciative glance at the fence again. "Next time tell him I've got a perfectly good fence up the road he can crash through."

He flung his hand out toward the new rails and posts. "Look at this! They reinforced and painted the whole dang thing." Smiling again, he nudged his son with his elbow while watching Allison. "You say he stayed here? Alone in the house with you? Do I need to have a talk with the young man?"

She felt herself blush. "Uncle John. I'm a nurse, for heaven's sake. Nursing is what he needed last night." *True enough. A nurse and more.* "I went to sleep in my own bed and he stayed in the office."

Fingers crossed behind her back, she waggled her brows at him. "Besides, I was safe, the shape he was in. If I'd wanted to have my way with him, he couldn't have fought me off." *And he didn't!*

"Aw, Allie, Dad didn't mean anything." Impossibly, Ned blushed deeper than she did.

They were the same age but by all indications, he was more backward in the way of love than she.

Which is really sad.

"I know, Ned." She smiled to ease his mind before taking a sip of coffee.

"Well, just so you know. We trust you." Ned walked to the driver side of the truck. "Wanna come home with us for a supper? I know Mom's fixed plenty."

John hung his head and shook it. "Boy needs a wife," he muttered.

"No, thanks, Ned. I've already eaten." Ned climbed in as Allison followed her uncle to the passenger door. She was surprised when he stopped and looked seriously at her.

"You know, Allie, no one would have been disappointed in you if something *had* happened last night. Guy makes up for an accident by doing all this"—he waved at the fence again—"well, he can't be too bad. Pretty girl like you should be with a man, having a family."

As simplistic as it sounded, that was how he understood life, for her as well as Ned. If only life was as easy as he saw it.

"Uncle John, I'm thirty-two. Hardly a girl, and only sweet people like you, who love me, consider me pretty. Between age and this limp, I'm sure I'm not what the average man is looking for."

He tapped her nose with his index finger. "That's your problem, Allie. For someone as good as you, we don't want an 'average' man. He'd better be a whole helluva lot better than average."

With a last look at Stuart Samuels' carpentry handiwork, he got in the truck and Ned pulled off.

Your Desire

Dee S. Knight

Chapter Five

Two long months had passed. Two months where she'd received two phone calls from David Wills, one asking if fence repairs had been made to her satisfaction and another the next week to find out how she was and whether there was anything she needed. Allison had assumed the interest had been Frank's although that wasn't clear.

She'd also received flowers—a dozen roses the first week, carnations the second, an orchid the third—something different every week, all with very polite thank you notes attached. The kind of gifts a secretary would be told to send. There was no word from Frank himself.

After the second week, she'd given up hope she would hear directly from him. Flowers were nice, but not when what she wanted was to hear him, his voice when he spoke her name, his tone when he said how he felt. He could have called and recited the latest stock report and she wouldn't have cared. But there was nothing. When she finally accepted that flowers were all she'd ever get from him again, her heart ached.

Foolish! Telling herself over and over didn't help at all. The plain fact of the matter was, despite her skepticism that such a thing could happen so fast, she'd been struck by love. Inexplicably, against all reason, undeniably hit hard.

In the dark, with the night hours stretched before her, she often relived Frank's touch on her skin, the feel of his lips coaxing her nipples erect, and the heart-stopping sensation of his being inside her, moving, stoking a fire only he knew how to put out. On those nights she would touch herself, rubbing her clit and imagining Frank's finger had brought her to completion. Or better, his luscious, full mouth.

But it wasn't the sex she missed most. It was the quiet companionship. The time they'd spent sharing their lives and the trust each expressed by their simple admissions of need. Of course, she hadn't told him about the accident, that had seemed too much. He would have pulled back from her knowing how imperfect she was. Most men saw. Not just that she wasn't a beauty, but her lack of grace and unbalanced walk. In his blindness, Frank had seen only her heart.

Finally, after weeks, Allison forced herself to acknowledge that her love was not only irrational, having little foundation, but also totally one-sided. He'd asked for a night, she'd done the same. Their time had been an experience beyond anything she could have hoped for, but she needed to move on.

The sticking point was how to do that. For the first time, she investigated options that weren't safe or comfortable. She thought about taking time off and traveling. She had the money. But spending time for pure pleasure didn't sit well; the need to be busy was too strongly ingrained. Still, she could take a few days and go to Washington, DC. In her mind, she saw herself passing Frank on the street. She'd smile and he'd…. He'd walk by because he wouldn't recognize the crazy woman smiling at him. No, a trip to Washington was out. She'd rather have the memories she carried than take a chance on damaging them.

Using the computer, Allison looked up every piece of information she could on NicHughes Electronics and its owner. His picture, taken a few years earlier, was on the corporation's website, but more recent photos were found in the Washington newspaper. Over the course of several years, she saw photos of Frank socializing with beautiful women as well as meeting business and government officials. She felt like a schoolgirl with a crush on a man impossibly above her station.

Then one night late in June, the phone rang.

"Mary! How great to hear from you. What's up?"

"Allison, I know you're going to want to kick me, but I have a *huge* favor to ask, and you *can't* say no. Tell me right now, you won't say no." She took a breath. "Hi, by the way. How are you?"

Allison had to laugh. "Fine. No need to ask how you are since I can tell you're in your usual tear. I won't say yes until I hear what the favor is," she teased.

"But you won't say no?"

"Spill the beans."

Deep breath. "We're having a special meeting to review the reunion. And discuss preliminary plans for the next one."

Allison groaned.

"I can't be there. Honestly, Allison, I would drop everything and drive down if I could, but Melissa's having a recital, and Michael is in a ballgame, and frankly, I can't keep up with everything going on at work now. Please say you'll represent me?"

She hesitated, then let out a frustrated sigh. "It's not fair using your children against me."

"Yes, I know. Sorry." She didn't really sound sorry, though.

"Just go to the meeting in your place? I don't have to volunteer for anything?"

"No volunteering. I'll send you all the paperwork relating to the weekend in April—which was a big success, by the way. I'm really sorry you missed so much of it."

The meeting sounded safe, although she had a feeling Mary wasn't telling her the full story. "Okay, I can help you out, I think. When is the meeting?"

"This weekend."

Allison snorted.

"I know," Mary agreed with a what-were-they-*thinking* tone. "Still, can you go?"

"Yes, no problem. Where is it, at the high school?"

Mary was quiet for a moment. When she spoke, Allison knew just how Mary's children felt when she was trying to persuade them to take medicine they knew would taste terrible.

"Nooo, at the country club. Out on the mountain. It'll be beautiful, won't it? And this is a dinner meeting, so they've reserved a room. Really, they're going all out. I'll bet it'll just be *fab*ulous, and here I'm going to have to miss it."

"What are you not telling me, Mary?"

"There is one little thing, but it's not really *that* important."

Mary took another deep breath. How bad was this request, anyway?

"Because the theme was so successful, we thought it would be fun to continue it all the way to the end. So everyone is wearing the same retro outfits they did for the dinner."

"No."

"Allis–"

"No! I'll be happy to represent you, but I won't wear that dress again. I'm surprised I haven't burned it." But she knew why she hadn't, why she'd keep the ugly thing forever.

"Okay, you're forcing me to tell you this. I didn't want to because I know how you are about causes. I've never known anyone in my life so dedicated to other people." Mary heaved a frustrated sigh. "You know we have several doctors in our class. Well, in the spirit of competition they started a bet. If we could get everyone at this meeting in the same outfits they wore that Saturday night, they'd donate time or money to a charity of our choice."

"Who would come up with something so stupid?"

"Adam Wilson, Zachary Barnes and Tommy Jensen. You know how they were in school and they haven't changed."

An idea formed in Allison's mind. Maybe she couldn't—wouldn't—take time for a long trip, but she could certainly handle a long weekend to visit a friend. In all the years Mary had lived in Baltimore, Allison had never been to see her, preferring instead to visit when Mary came home to see her family. It had been selfish of Allison, really. But now she could make up for it and make a change in her own life, too.

"Okay."

"What? I didn't quite hear you."

She could picture Mary sitting straight in astonishment, frowning at the telephone, and wondering why Allison had given in so quickly.

"I said, okay. I'll go to the meeting and I'll wear the damn dress." Smiling at the sound of relief on the other end, Allison added, "But you have to pay for this favor, pal. I want an invitation to Baltimore. I want to come up for a long weekend and be shown all the sights. Wining and dining, not necessary, but tours are."

"But I've asked you to come up dozens of times! *Wonderful!* When?"

"To be decided. All right, give me all the gory details about the reunion committee."

When she hung up, plans for the aquarium, the harbor tour and a quick trip antiquing in Annapolis far out shadowed the task of the weekend meeting. After all, the meeting was really just dinner, and with people she'd known practically forever. She'd show up with a little attitude and enjoy the evening *regardless* of her marital status, that she still lived in her hometown, or how she looked in her very plaid, noisy dress. Maybe she'd slip into the lounge after the meeting and see if there were dancing. If so, she'd *dance*. If no one asked her, she'd take the initiative.

The thought was daring, frightening, and maybe a little ambitious for her first venture out. But she knew it was time she started living a little. And damn anyone who thought otherwise.

*

Allison handed her keys to the valet and strolled to the deck rather than entering the building through the front. This was the kind of night her dress had been designed for, warm, almost sultry. The rustling of the fabric rivaled the sough of the breeze through the trees, and in the twilight the plaid of the full skirt became more subtle. She'd brought a light shawl in case the room was chilly, but outside a wrap wasn't necessary. Closing her eyes, she breathed deeply and let the final rays of sunlight warm her face.

The evening breeze was unusually warm. Not for the time of year, but for the elevation and hour. House Mountain Country Club sat on the side of a tree-covered mountain a few miles outside the city. The drive up to the club was steep and long, which made the view off the cantilevered deck all the more breathtaking.

The sun was low in the western sky but hadn't fallen behind the expanse of Blue Ridge Mountains. The eastern hillside, bathed in golden light, made the green needles of the pines, the distinctive leaves of the sycamore and redbud, and the shiny leaves of the mountain laurel shimmer as they turned in the light wind. Trees and bushes to the west were shrouded in the shadows of dusk and marked with subtle shadings of green and brown, soon to lose all unique characterization.

Ever since her conversation with Mary she'd looked forward to the evening with a mixture of trepidation and excitement. Earlier, she'd shed the dread as she put on the dress. Strangely, suddenly she'd anticipated the evening, determining to make a difference in her life. Taking the advice she'd given Frank, she'd decided to forget all about others and think only of herself, just for tonight.

The determination held and now she was ready to face her peers. She turned and walked into the building.

The reunion committee was scheduled in the Laurel Room. As she approached, she saw people milling around outside the door, some with drinks, others simply standing and chatting before dinner. All wore the attire she remembered from a couple of months ago, and she smiled thinking that the Doctors Wilson, Barnes and Jensen would indeed be paying for this prank.

Her smile must have been warm, because Harry McDonnell, the chairman of the committee smiled back. "Allison, Mary told me you'd be here." He glanced quickly to the closed door of the room. "You're just a little early. They're still setting up."

She looked around at the crowd. "Gosh, Harry, there are a lot of people here, aren't there? And I see quite a few people from town here who weren't in our class. There must be some other meeting taking place tonight."

"Yes, there must be something special going on." Harry looked pleased with himself as he sipped his drink. "Can I get you something from the bar?"

"Oh, no thanks." She held up a manila folder. "Mary sent me the figures you'll need, but I didn't expect there to be this many people in attendance to discuss them."

He shrugged. "I just passed the word that we'd be here, and a lot of people said they wanted to get together again."

"Yes," she murmured, paying closer attention to who was there. Sammy Mayer who lived in Roanoke, and Meryl Williams who lived in Raleigh. Surely that was a bit far to come for an impromptu class meeting?

"You look real nice tonight, Allison. Those colors suit you. I meant to tell you in April, but by the time we got in and settled, you'd already gone."

Eyes wide with surprise, she flashed him another smile. "Thanks, Harry. I appreciate it." She reached for the door handle. "If you don't mind, I'll just find my place before we all crowd in."

"I don't think—"

She hardly heard his protest as she swept through the doorway and into the quiet room. Astonished, she looked at the number of tables set up for dinner. A quick count showed twenty tables with eight places each. This was a replay of their reunion, not a business meeting. At the front of the room was a microphone fronted with pots of flowers. A man in a black suit, no doubt one of the staff, seemed to be arranging place cards on the front table.

Slowly, her dress swishing around her legs in the way she almost no longer noticed, she passed the tables looking for her place. The man straightened as she approached.

"Hello, Allison."

With a gasp she stopped. The black suit was a tuxedo. The staff person was Frank, as she clearly saw when he turned to face her. There was a hesitant smile on his lips.

She stepped back, into a chair. "Frank! Wh-what are you doing here?"

Her dress fit too tightly suddenly, as she tried to catch her breath. Even without a mirror she knew how pale she was because she literally felt the blood leave her face. *God, please don't let me faint. Or cry, Lord, please.*

"Would you be surprised to know I'm supposed to be here?"

"Yes."

His smile widened as he examined her, head to toe and back again, slowly. The confidence she'd adopted since dressing flowed out of her with his scrutiny.

"You can see."

He focused on her face, and she remembered the pictures in the newspaper of the beautiful women he'd escorted to events in Washington. She'd never felt so lacking.

"Yes, I can. But only for the last eight days. Your doctors were right."

He stepped forward, blocking the exit she'd frantically started to plan.

"And I'm awfully glad I can, because now I see you." Lifting his hand, he reached out but then pulled back.

Was he nervous? With *her*?

Heat infused her cheeks as blood rushed back into her face. She quickly looked at the toes of her slippers peeking out from the hem of her dress. "I'm not, but it's very nice of you to say so."

There was no hesitance now. With a tender touch, he tilted her head back so their eyes met. She saw a frown where a moment ago had been a smile.

"Please don't argue with me on this. I didn't come here for an argument." His voice was even better than she remembered. Deep and low, it caressed her.

"Why did you come here?" she whispered.

The doors opened and the people who had been filling the hall poured into the room. Frank glanced up then took her arm, leading her to the other side of the table. "You're here," he said, placing her behind a chair very close to the microphone. "And since you saw me moving the place cards, you know it's no coincidence that I'm here." Standing behind the chair next to hers, he flashed her a smile that made her heart stop.

Her surprise increased when Mary moved to stand on her other side. She giggled at Allison's shock. "We managed to surprise you this time, didn't we?"

"What is going on here, Mary?" She croaked the question. In a fit of nerves, her fingers clutched the back of the chair and tension sent spears of pain shooting from her lower back down her leg.

"You'll see." Mary leaned forward. "Mr. Hughes, have you met Allison Hayes?"

Frank grinned at Allison then at Mary. "Yes, I have. Thank you for rescheduling this event, Mrs. Simpson. I wouldn't have wanted to miss being part of the celebration."

"Mary, I'm not happy about–"

Mary tapped her wine glass with a knife, effectively quieting the room. Frank pulled Allison's chair out as Mary slipped behind them and went to the microphone.

"Let me start by saying thank you so much for coming back to Lexington tonight. An unfortunate set of events prevented us from the presentation in April, but I think all will go well tonight. Just in case, does anyone have the numbers for the fire department, EMT and police?" Laughter flowed through the audience.

"We're not taking any chances this time, finishing business before we enjoy dinner." She waited a moment until everyone's attention was focused on her again. "Now, the last time we met, our guest of honor disappeared on us." Mary shot Allison a stern look. "Not her fault, though, because she didn't know she was the guest of honor. As it turned out, it was a good thing she left us early because some fool man had run his car through her fence and needed all kinds of care."

Frank reached under the tablecloth and grasped Allison's hand.

"And men say women don't know how to drive." Good natured laughter again filtered through the room. "Naturally, our Allison generously did all she could, even taking the man home when he refused to stay in the hospital. Such is her nature, and the reason we're all here." The room burst into applause.

Allison's head began to ache and her back worsened.

"As it turned out, our presenter that night had an emergency of his own, in the form of an eight-and-a-half-pound baby boy." Mary waited for a smattering of talk to die down. "Tonight, we are very honored to play host to the founder and CEO of one of the largest electronics firms in America. What's not so well known is that he's also the founder of Helping Hands. Please welcome Mr. Nicholas Hughes." She stepped back from the microphone, clapping her hands and beaming at Frank.

He squeezed Allison's hand before letting go and standing to acknowledge the recognition. When he moved to the microphone, Mary returned to her chair, ignoring Allison's perplexed look.

"Thank you, Mrs. Simpson. Ladies and gentlemen, I'm very pleased to be here tonight. In fact, I knew Martin Johnson had rescheduled this presentation and I *insisted* on coming here to do the honors. And I'll tell you why." He looked squarely at Allison. "I wanted to see such a special person with my own eyes."

Tears threatened her. Frank continued talking but she hardly heard a word. With astonishment, she determined that she was being honored, but for what she wasn't quite sure. The things Frank mentioned about her didn't seem so extraordinary. *Do they give awards for simply living your life?* Apparently so.

Somehow she stood and accepted a check for ten thousand dollars and the plaque Frank produced. She managed a weak, "I don't know what to say. Thank you," before he escorted her the few steps back to the table. She stared in amazement as the people she'd known for years stood to honor her.

Grasping the plaque to her like a support line, she smiled through her tears at her former classmates and friends. These were the very people among whom she'd felt like such an oddity only a couple of months earlier. Now, she didn't know how to feel.

Finally, thankfully, they sat, and dinner was served. Her meal was interrupted so much by people stopping to read the tribute on the rosewood plaque and to chat, she finally gave up and pushed her plate away.

Frank, ignoring blatant flirtations from some of the women, never left her side, touching her shoulder as he stood to greet person after person, leaning slightly to rub arms as he encouraged her to eat a little more, lightly caressing her neck as they enjoyed coffee and conversation after dinner.

When a decent amount of time had passed and people started to leave, Frank whispered that if she was ready he'd escort her home. She nodded, and he left to have their cars brought around.

After fiercely hugging Mary, Allison gave her a mock glare. "You and I *will* have a discussion about this, Mary Simpson." Then she smiled. "What a wonderful friend you are. Thank you. I'm overwhelmed."

"You deserve this and more. I'm so glad Jeff Waters read about the Helping Hands foundation. When he mentioned it at a meeting last year as something we should investigate, there was only one person's name who came to everyone's lips. You should *see* the letters we got about you. You've touched a lot of lives for one so young." Mary fluffed her hair and batted her eyelashes in a mock flirt. "I added that last bit because we're the same age."

Allison laughed.

Mary dropped her voice. "Allie, have you met Nicholas Hughes before tonight? He seems awfully familiar with you."

She felt herself blush. "We did meet once. I had no idea who he was."

"Well, he likes you. A lot, if the way he acted tonight is any indication." She pursed her lips and quirked her brows. "Isn't he a little out of our league?"

For the first time since seeing Frank standing in the Laurel Room, Allison felt her stress disappear. She laughed. "Nope. *We* may be out of *his*." Holding up the check and grinning, she added, "Maybe he's after me for my money. I'll let you know." With a flounce of flowing, rustling skirts, she spun and hurried out to find Frank.

Chapter Six

"I hope you're not too tired. I really need to talk to you." He'd parked behind her Jeep, then moved beside her at the foot of her porch steps. Just being there, breathing her scent, feeling her warmth as well as her strength in the arm he lightly held, sent a paroxysm of lust through him. Funny, that. Probably because he'd fallen for her sight unseen, it was the non-visual cues that were jetting his libido into overdrive. Not that he wasn't pleased with everything he saw, too. Allison was a beautiful woman.

"No, I'm not too tired. Would you like some coffee?"

No. I want you. "Sure, that would be fine."

Great conversation, Hughes. It's a wonder she's not tripping all over herself to get to you.

The minute he'd seen her that evening his heart rose to his throat and jammed there. Only years of negotiating had allowed him to appear in charge when in fact he was ready to chew his nails. He wasn't a man given to nervousness, certainly not over women. But then he'd never wanted anyone before like he wanted Allison.

No one had ever occupied his thoughts and dreams as she had. If the blindness had cleared up sooner, he'd have been back for her long before now, but he couldn't talk himself into coming before he was healed. It wouldn't be fair, he'd told himself for weeks, to ask her to accept him as anything less than perfect—or as perfect as he could be. As it was, the stress of wanting her probably exacerbated the condition, which continued to keep him away. Circular logic in a comedy of errors directed by Fate.

Into the second month, he'd been ready to do anything, even beg her to accept him, regardless of his being blind. When he realized he wanted her that much, he knew he'd been a fool to wait so long. Panicked she might have forgotten him, he tried to think of a way to come back into her life without seeming pathetic and needy. Then he heard the award had been rescheduled. Assuming the role of presenter, he'd called Mary Simpson to set the whole thing up. Still blind but more in love than a man had a right to be, he prepared himself to face Allison once more, still blind. Amazingly, the next week his sight had returned.

Which wouldn't count for shit if he found now that he was in a one-sided relationship, a possibility causing him a great deal of worry.

Tossing his jacket over the back of a kitchen chair, he pulled his tie loose and unbuttoned the collar button. He turned a chair around and straddled it, crossing his arms on the back. She bustled around in what he could see was a modern farm kitchen—open, large, and very efficiently laid out—looking at anything but him, and making that wonderful swishing sound with every movement.

"I love that dress," he said, closing his eyes to concentrate on the sound. To his surprise, he couldn't pinpoint her location in the room, even hearing her. "But for some reason, I can't keep up with you like I could before."

"That's because you don't need to anymore. You can use your eyes to see what you want."

Opening his eyes, he was happy to see her regarding him. "Yes, I sure can, can't I?"

She blushed under his gaze.

"This is the fourth or fifth time tonight you've blushed. Did you embarrass this easily when I was here a couple of months ago?"

Laughing, she finished pouring water into the pot. "No, I don't think so. You couldn't see me, so it was easier to say and do things without feeling judged." She pushed the On button to start the brew cycle. "Plus, I didn't think I'd ever see you again. That gives a person even more freedom."

"Why didn't you think you'd see me again?" Tilting his head, he rested his chin on his arms.

"Well, you were here for a specific reason and when that ended, our purpose in being together ended, too. Then there's the matter of our coming from two different worlds." She smiled. "Lastly, you'd made sure the fence was fixed, so there was no need for me to contact you about it."

"That fence again," he said with a feigned growl.

"If you'd left it broken, I would have had to call and threaten all kinds of legal action until you fixed it. I could have found out how you were then." She removed a carton of cream from the refrigerator, then put it and the sugar bowl on the counter near two ceramic cups. "My uncle and cousin were most impressed with the work, and that you would do so much to make up for what was obviously an accident. I appreciated it, too." She leaned against the counter. "I'm glad you got the NASA contract. I'm sure you were happy."

He wanted to get past her polite tone, needed her to remember the fire they'd had before. Even the emotion that resulted from the shock of seeing him at the country club would be preferable to this guest treatment.

"I was, yes. How did you know we got it?"

She looked away, acting like she was checking the progress of the coffee maker. "Oh, I must have seen it in the paper."

Something wasn't right. Why wouldn't she look at him? He played a hunch. "The Washington paper?"

"Hmm, might have been." Reaching out to jiggle the pot she frowned. "What's taking this thing so long?"

"You read the Washington paper to find out about me, didn't you?"

Facing him, her chin set in a stubborn pose, she said, "I suppose I did. I was interested, knowing you and all."

Ah! She hadn't forgotten about him, not for a minute. He could feel it. But he wanted to hear her say it. "I'm very glad you were curious about me. Why didn't you call?"

She snorted. "Let me ask the same of you."

He tried to meet her eyes, but she turned toward the damn coffee pot again. Couldn't she tell he didn't give a rat's ass about coffee? "I *couldn't* call you, not until—"

"Thanks for all the flowers, by the way. They weren't necessary." Changing the subject when he was trying to get personal could be good or bad. His heart began a steadily increasing thump.

He stood and walked across the room, bracing his hands on the counter and bracketing her with his arms. Her rich, brown eyes darkened with his closeness and her breath hitched. The satiny smoothness of the dress brushed his skin as she tried to edge away, but he stepped forward, making her space as much his as he could.

"They *were* necessary. If I'd been able to write the notes myself, they would have said what I felt, what was in my heart, not the impersonal things I'm sure my admin felt obliged to write."

If ever there was a time for nerves of steel, this was it. He grasped the counter tighter to keep her from knowing how unsteady his hands were.

"I couldn't tell her to spell out that you were never out of my mind, that every night I went to sleep thinking of how you felt in my arms. How much I missed *having* you in my arms." He leaned down to kiss her, a brief touch of lips. "Until I knew if you felt the same, I was too afraid to say those things. And until I could see, I didn't have the courage to come and find out if you felt the same."

Were those tears in her eyes? Oh, God! The worst had happened. He'd gotten up the nerve to tell her his feelings and she was so upset she was crying.

"It's okay, Allison. Don't feel embarrassed. I guess I know now what I came to find out." He started to pull away.

"Wait!"

Frank studied her, hoping he hid the fear that she would confirm in words what she'd shown silently with her tears. He didn't want to listen to her explain why there was no need for him to hang around.

She pushed out of his arms and walked away. "Frank, I didn't hear a word from you. Flowers from your secretary and phone calls from your assistant, but nothing from you, for two months. How could you do that and then come here expecting me to fall into your arms?"

"I'm sorry. I'm so sorry, Allison." Coming up behind her, he took a breath to formulate exactly what to say. "I was stubborn, I guess. I wanted you with everything in me, but I couldn't bear to ask you to accept me handicapped."

He saw her stiffen and placed his hands on her shoulders, then lightly ran them down her arms, catching her hands and wrapping them at her waist. "I knew you would, you see, because by then I knew who you are and that you love lost causes. I couldn't stand the thought that you would come to me simply because you wanted to help.

"That was at the beginning. I thought when we were on equal footing, then I'd call and ask you to see me again. I couldn't do it before then, don't you see? To hear your voice and not be able to tell you how I felt, what I wanted, would have been awful."

He heard her sigh, felt her muscles relax. "I'd just decided that being without you was worse than having my stupid pride, when I found out about the ceremony. I was determined to be here tonight come hell or high water, blind or not, and find out how you feel about me, with all my imperfections. Then the contract came through and my eyesight returned all in the same jumbled mess. I'm so sorry I hurt you. Can you forgive me?"

She fell back against his chest, leaning into him. "So you came here tonight to find out how I feel about you?"

"Yes." Should he say it first or wait for her? He loved her, damn it, but what if she didn't love him?

"I can't believe you're saying these things to me."

For the second time in minutes his heart sank. She didn't feel as he did, struck by a wild emotion that had knocked him off his feet. It had all been on his part.

"Love at first sight is a fairy tale, a romantic myth that never happens to anyone, really. So how did it happen to us?"

For a moment, what she'd said didn't penetrate the fog in his brain. "You mean you *do* feel something for me?" Despair turned to elation in milliseconds. He wanted to shout, dance, tell the world that this amazing, wonderful woman loved him, even with his weaknesses and flaws. He was the luckiest man alive. Suddenly he couldn't stop smiling.

"Something? Much more than 'something.' I can't believe you feel anything for *me*. I mean…." Turning in his arms she closed her eyes, seeming to reach for the right words. "Being without you taught me a few things about myself. Things that I need to change in my life. But I'm not sure those changes can involve us."

The smile disappeared. "What are you talking about?" His tone was sharp, but he couldn't stand any more of this roller coaster of emotion. "I love you, Allison." To hell with waiting for her to say it. It was time to put his cards on the table.

Opening her eyes, she reached up to touch his face. "You only like perfection, Frank, you said so. And I'm the one who's handicapped, as you can now see."

Taking her hand to his lips he kissed her palm. "Why would you say that? When I turned around after hearing that beautiful, wonderful noise this dress makes, I couldn't believe my eyes. That your physical beauty would match the person I already knew you to be seemed too much to hope for. Allison, there isn't anything about you that isn't perfect."

"Not true. I'm not pretty, I know that. But I have scars, I-I limp. There's nothing graceful about me. You don't know me, not really."

"Scars, a limp? What are they compared to who you are? And I know a great deal more about you than you might think. My foundation doesn't hand out money without pretty thoroughly investigating the prospect. Stupid me, when I came here the last time, I hadn't looked at the plaque and didn't know who it was going to. David had to tell me who you were. When I got home, I had Martin fill me in on everything he'd discovered. I know about the accident, Allison."

She flinched.

He pulled her closer, tucking her head against his heart. "We got letter after letter explaining how horrible the fall was, how you almost died, then how the surgeries left you scarred, physically but a bit emotionally, too. Funny, I never noticed a limp when I was here before, and we walked side by side. If I hadn't been looking, I wouldn't have noticed it tonight. That's because like most people, I'll bet, I was looking at your beautiful face. How your eyes sparkle with warmth and life."

She shook her head against his shirt.

"Yes! You don't know how many people told us what an example you were, of your courage through everything, how you made friends and shared, always, with those who had less than you. We heard from people at the battered women's shelter and the literacy group—do you have any idea how many people could even write their letters to us because of help you gave them?—and from shut-ins who look forward to your visit and conversation even more than the hot lunches you bring. Don't even get me started on your colleagues from the hospital and former patients.

"But I didn't need any of that to know I already loved you. In the one night we were together, you taught me I could let go. That sometimes it's okay not to be in control, that I could trust myself to someone else and not be weakened. You don't know what a relief it was. You had pain and needs that night and yet you were willing to do everything for me, to give me strength to lean on. Do you have any idea how important that was?"

Again she shook her head.

"When I got home my staff closed around me like a phalanx. I would never have asked for help, but they must have sensed that I was changed somehow, and they literally closed ranks. That *never* would have happened before my night with you. You changed my life, all because you gave me your trust and accepted mine. I love you."

"Are you sure your feelings aren't coming just from the sex, Frank? Or from misplaced feelings for your nurse? That happens, you know." Tears streamed down her face.

He wiped them off with hands that no longer trembled with nervousness. "Very sure."

"I love you, too," she whispered.

He crushed her against him, certain he felt tears in his eyes, now. "Do you think the town is going to hate me for taking you away?

Because I want to marry you, but I have to live a little closer to business."

"I think they'll understand," she answered with a short laugh.

"Good." He took her lips in another gentle kiss and let it grow as she pressed into him. His tongue traced the seam of her mouth and she opened to him. He loved that her tongue immediately touched his.

He dropped his arm to her side, smoothing his hand on the fabric covering her thigh. "Is your leg bothering you?" he asked in a voice hoarse with longing.

Shaking her head she said, "No, I'm fine." She tried to kiss him again.

Leaning back, he gazed into her eyes. "I just thought maybe you needed to get off your feet." He saw the moment his meaning dawned on her.

With a look of complete innocence, she grazed her hand along his inner thigh until she caressed his raging hard-on. "Do you feel the need to get off your feet?"

"You know it." The kiss he gave her was hard and fast. "Are you still on birth control?"

"I never was."

"What?" His heart stopped as he recalled their making love without condoms.

She looked chagrined. "What was done was done. I wanted to be with you. There wasn't any reason to add to your worries, and I would have dealt with anything that happened."

He opened his mouth, but she answered the question before he asked. "As it turned out, nothing happened. I would have told you if it had, I promise."

He could barely speak, he wanted her so. "You're going to marry me, aren't you?"

"Yes, I want to marry you."

Thank God! "And children?" He whispered against her lips.

"Your children? Yes, I'd love to have children."

It was as though a sun burst inside him, filling him with heat. "I do love you, Allison."

With a smile more seductive than he'd seen on any other woman's face, she murmured, "If I could only find someone to help me get out of this dress."

His chuckle was low. "I can help you with that." Reaching around, he untied the strap at the back of her neck then unzipped the lower bodice. The dress pooled in a soft rustle at her feet.

He drank in the sight of her.

"There's so much more I want to know," she said, "about you and about us."

"Later, sweetheart. Right now, I just want to enjoy the magic."

She smiled as he lifted her and carried her to the kitchen table. In seconds he divested her of panties and hose. Closing his eyes, he leaned his head on her stomach and slipped his finger between her legs. She was wet and ready for him, which made him smile with wonder. He unzipped his trousers and released his cock, engorged and just as ready for her.

"It is magic," he groaned, pushing into her, losing himself in the perfume of their mixed desire and the touch of her fingers. This was home, this was where he belonged.

"Yes, magic," she whispered. Her fingers tangled in his hair as she pulled him down for a kiss. "I'll never disbelieve again."

* * * *

"Well, that turned out very nicely, indeed," said Nigel as he matched two pieces of material and pinned them.

"How do you even know what happened?" asked Edwina. "You weren't watching from the window."

He spared her a brief smile. "That comes with age and experience. I could feel that they'd finally gotten together."

Edwina twisted her hands and frowned.

He laid the material on the table in order to focus on his granddaughter. She looked younger than she had in weeks, in pigtails—purple and green, of course, but he was almost starting to enjoy her frequent color changes—and coveralls. "What's wrong?"

She took a breath. "Gramps, they were...you know...doing it on the *table*. That's so gross."

Nigel chuckled and picked up the material again. "Yes, I suppose you'd see it that way. But you might not always. Love is strange sometimes, my dear."

"Well, I hope the people in Iowa are a bit more discriminating," she said, sounding so priggish Nigel had to laugh.

"One can always hope."

Thanks for reading!

Thanks so much for taking the time to read my fantasy! As you probably know, many people look at reviews on Amazon and/or Goodreads before they decide to make a purchase. If you liked this book could you please take a minute to leave a review and give your feedback?

About the author

A few years ago, Dee S. Knight began writing, making getting up in the morning fun. During the day, her characters killed people, fell in love, became drunk with power, or sober with responsibility. And they had sex, lots of sex. She is the primary persona of three pen names—triplets, if you will: Dee, Anne Krist, and Jenna Stewart.

As noted above, Dee S. Knight writes erotic romance—emphasis on the romance! "Sister" Anne does not write erotic romance. Her book, Burning Bridges, has received high praise and multiple 5-star reviews because of the depth of the romance and emotion. Third of the triplets, Jenna has tried her hand at ménage—in both historical and shifter books

Regardless of the name she uses to write during the day, their dream man, childhood sweetheart, and long-time hubby are all the same guy. What happens during their nights are their secret.

For romance ranging from sweet to historical, contemporary to paranormal and more, join the girls on www.NomadAuthors.com. Sign up for Dee's newsletter with Jan Selbourne and have access to fun free reads.

Also, we have a blog with weekly posts featuring interesting articles and interviews with some of your favorite authors. In addition, once a month, look for Charity Sunday blog posts where your comment can support a selected charity. Our blog site is found at www.nomadauthors.com/blog.

Books

By Dee S. Knight:

Naval Maneuvers
Only a Good Man Will Do, Book 1 of the Good Man series
One Woman Only, Book 2 of the Good Man series
Passionate Destiny

Dee S. Knight

The Triple S Bride
The Bride of the Pryde
        By Anne Krist (non-erotic romance)
Burning Bridges
        By Jenna Stewart (Historical ménage and -Shifters)
The Sisters O'Ryan series
Strange Bedfellows series
The Great Wolves of Men-Edge series

www.ingramcontent.com/pod-product-compliance
Lightning Source LLC
Chambersburg PA
CBHW070802200626
46811CB00023B/442